WEDDING
THE GREEK
BILLIONAIRE

WEDDING THE GREEK BILLIONAIRE

REBECCA WINTERS

MILLS & BOON

First published in Great Britain 2018
by Mills & Boon, an imprint of HarperCollins*Publishers*
1 London Bridge Street, London, SE1 9GF

Large Print edition 2019

© 2018 Rebecca Winters

ISBN: 978-0-263-08201-2

MIX
Paper from
responsible sources
FSC™ C007454

This book is produced from independently certified
FSC™ paper to ensure responsible forest management.
For more information visit www.harpercollins.co.uk/green.

Printed and bound in Great Britain
by CPI Group (UK) Ltd, Croydon, CR0 4YY

I've been so thrilled with my editor, I want to dedicate this book to her. Thank you for believing in me, working with me, helping me to be better. Every author needs the right editor to make her work stronger. Some authors are lucky enough to have an editor who also has a great personality, who's pleasant, understanding, fun, kind and supportive, as well as being an expert in bringing out the best in her writing. I have an editor like that. Thank you, Julia.

CHAPTER ONE

THE END OF May had brought glorious seventy-degree weather to Greece, but the morning traffic in Patras was as bad as in Athens. Zoe Perkins, who'd been in Greece since January, doing research on the renowned British poet Lord Byron, was on her way to the dock in a taxi. The ferry to Ithaca would be leaving soon and she couldn't be late.

"Can't you go any faster?" she called to the driver again. She'd phoned for a taxi from her one bedroom apartment in downtown Patras, thinking she had plenty of time.

"I am hurrying," he replied in English over his shoulder.

She looked out the window, frustrated it was taking so long. Suddenly she saw a truck turn into their path from the intersection. "Stop! He's going to hit—"

They collided before she could say *us*. The impact shot her forward, but the seat belt kept her from going flying. While she tried to get her heart to calm down, she noticed the driver slumped over the steering wheel. Blood dribbled down the side of his face.

"Oh, no! Are you all right?" she cried out, horrified. He didn't make a sound. It was her fault for urging him to drive faster. The police hadn't arrived yet and a crowd had surrounded them. The accident had caused a terrible traffic jam.

Galvanized into action, Zoe undid the seat belt, wanting to get out of the car to help the driver. But as she opened the rear door, she was blocked by a man with a rock-hard physique saying something to her in Greek.

"Please let me out."

"I'm sorry, *kyria*, but you might need medical attention. Help is coming." The man's deep cultured voice spoken in accented English was disturbingly attractive.

"Thank you, but I'm fine. Honestly! The driver is the one who's hurt. I tried talking to him, but he isn't saying anything!"

When he lowered his head, she found herself staring at the most striking, olive-skinned Greek male she'd ever seen in her life. Beneath raven-black hair and brows, his eyes, dark as midnight, studied her features as if to verify she'd spoken the truth.

The thirty-plus-looking male was dressed in an elegant tan silk suit and tie. She assumed he had to be on his way to an important meeting.

"Why don't we let the paramedics decide." He didn't move, and spoke in a tone of authority he probably wasn't even aware of.

"The poor man."

"He's already sitting up, *kyria*, and has likely broken his nose, nothing else."

"I—I shouldn't have told him to drive so fast." Shock was setting in, causing her to chatter. "I was afraid I'd miss the f-ferry for Ithaca."

"Was someone going to meet you when you arrived?"

"No, it's just I was on a tight schedule and there won't be another one until tomorrow. But it doesn't matter now because the driver is hurt. He needs help."

"He'll be fine. Just try to relax."

At that moment she heard a siren and the paramedics arrived. They appeared to recognize the stranger immediately. He spoke to them briefly, then moved aside so one of them could talk to her in English. The medic checked her vital signs while the taxi driver received help and was transported to the ambulance.

Determining that she seemed to be all right, the medic helped her out of the taxi. All that time, the stranger stayed beside her. Zoe hadn't realized he was so tall, at least six feet two inches of male virility. Maybe the accident had affected her sight, because to her eyes he looked like a Greek god come to life. Her legs felt like mush.

The medic took her information and said he

would summon another taxi for her. Before she could answer him, the stranger said, "I'll drive her to her destination."

"*Efkaristo*, Kyrie Gavras."

Gavras? She'd passed the entrance of a hotel downtown called Gavras House, Patras, many times. Was *he* that Gavras? Zoe had also seen the name in the news and everywhere she'd been in western Greece during her time here.

"You and I haven't been officially introduced, Kyria Perkins." The mention of her name meant he'd heard the information she'd given to the medic. "My name is Andreas Gavras. If you'll allow me, I'll take you where you need to go. My limo is waiting."

"Thank you, but you don't owe me anything."

"My driver was right behind the truck that collided with your taxi. I'm the one who called for assistance and would like to be of help. Wouldn't you do the same for me if our positions were reversed? Where can I take you?"

Think, Zoe. "Maybe back to my apartment. It's only a few blocks away."

He reached inside for her purse and handed it to her.

"Thank you." She'd forgotten she'd left it on the seat.

"The limo is parked just over there." He cupped her elbow to steady her as they walked through the stalled cars and he helped her into the back of the elegant black limo. "Do you feel ill?"

"Not sick, just shaken."

"Of course. What you need is a drink." He said something in Greek to his driver through a speaker, and the limo began to move. The next thing she knew they'd rounded a corner and pulled up in front of a sidewalk café.

"Stay right here, *kyria*. I'll be back."

In a lithe male movement, he got out of the limo and went inside. Before long he came back out with two drinks in paper cups. "This is lemonade."

Her hand trembled as she took the cup from him. "Thank you so much," she said before drinking thirstily. When she'd drained all of it, he took the cup from her and put it in a recep-tacle. He'd finished his drink, as well.

"I've never tasted anything so good."

"I'm glad it appealed. Feel a little better now?" he asked solicitously.

"Much." He was the proverbial white knight, but dressed in a stunning modern silk suit, who'd come out of nowhere to save her.

"Forgive me for a minute while I call my of-fice, then we'll find a pleasant place to have lunch."

"You've been very kind, but you look like you're on your way to an important meeting. Please don't let me keep you."

He slanted her a heart-stopping glance. "I'm glad you're the reason I can't make the board meeting I usually sleep through." She didn't be-lieve that for a second. "Besides, I have to eat since I didn't stop for breakfast this morning. Did you?"

"Actually I didn't. I thought I'd eat on the ferry."

"Well, I know a place where the food will be much better. Just give me a minute."

By the time he'd gotten off the phone, she felt her more normal self. Once again the limo joined the mainstream of traffic and drove them out of the city to the coast ten miles away.

"I'm in the mood for fish. How about you?"

"That sounds wonderful." But she didn't feel hungry.

"When we get there, shall I order for you?"

"Please. I haven't mastered your menus yet."

He spoke to his driver again and they pulled up to one of those seaside places you read about in a brochure for this century's jet set, exclusive and expensive. The restaurant was full, but a table had been reserved for them. He must have called ahead when he'd bought the lemonade.

Zoe knew she wasn't dreaming, but it felt like she was in one. He helped her to her seat and sat across from her at the cloth-covered table with flowers. After the waiter took their order, his black eyes studied her features.

"Why were you going to Ithaca?"

"Since January, I've been doing research in Greece on the life of George Gordon Noel Byron, the Sixth Baron Byron, known as Lord Byron. I've visited many places and been to many sites, but there are still regions I have yet to see and learn about."

To her surprise, his expression grew more animated. "Why him particularly?"

"He spent some time in and around Ithaca. I want to go there and talk to some of the local historians who will give me their insights about him."

"What kind of work do you do?"

"I'm studying for my doctorate at UCLA, and I teach classes on the romance writers of the early nineteenth century. Last Christmas a famous female movie director in Hollywood named Magda Collier started making her most important film to date and chose Lord Byron for the subject. She needed new eyes for fresh research to make the script authentic."

"And you were picked?"

"Two other women from Stanford and San

Jose State University, Ginger and Abby, plus myself, were chosen to gather material. Magda's idea was to show him as a genius whose spiritual side had so much to give the world and emphasize the greatness in him. I applauded her dream and was thrilled to be part of her team."

"That's quite an honor."

"In a way, it is. Before Christmas we met in Los Angeles for a week with the screenwriters and learned from her what she wanted. I've been sending information to her for months, as have my friends. But the time is coming when I'll have to return to the US, so I'm trying to make the most of it."

"It sounds like you were an expert on him to begin with."

"I've studied his works for years and have learned incredible things about his life while he spent time here in Greece."

"How long have you been in Patras?"

"About six weeks."

Their food came and it looked delicious, whetting her appetite. She ended up feasting on a plate of all sorts of fish and rice in a divine cream sauce.

"This is delicious, but I feel guilty that the poor taxi driver is probably at the hospital in pain. If he has a family, they must be so upset this happened."

"Your compassion is commendable."

"I'm sure you'd feel the same way. Do you think it was his fault?"

"I'm not sure, but I can find out what hospital he was taken to. Maybe then we might learn details."

"Would you do that? If I could, I'd like to tell him how sorry I am for what happened. I've relied on taxis all through Greece. The drivers have always been wonderful and I've been so lucky. It astounds me how well they speak English. If I had to drive a Greek person around, I wouldn't be able to communicate. It's shameful that I only know a few words after all these months."

"Not everyone is as appreciative as you. I'm

impressed, *kyria*, and I'll see what I can do on our way back to Patras."

"Thank you."

"Would you care for dessert?"

"I couldn't manage one, but please order for yourself if you want to."

"I'd rather drive you back to Patras while we find out about your taxi driver so you can relax."

"I'm sorry."

"You have nothing to apologize for. An accident that was out of your hands would unnerve anyone."

He summoned the waiter and they left the restaurant for the limo. They sat across from each other as they'd done before. On the way into town he got on his cell phone and made a series of calls. Zoe knew that if anyone could pull strings to find out private information, he would be the one.

"I have good news," he said after hanging up on his last call. "The driver received a cut on his eyebrow that was stitched up. He's already been released from the hospital."

"That's a great relief to me. I'm glad it wasn't his nose."

Her knight chuckled. "The driver of the truck wasn't injured. He was given the citation for not being careful."

"I can't thank you enough for finding out that information for me. I'll sleep much better tonight."

By this time the limo had pulled up in front of her apartment without needing directions. When the stranger had heard her give the police her information, he'd clearly remembered the address.

"What are your plans now?" he asked.

"Work. I'll make use of today's loss of time by transcribing some tapes I've made during interviews here. Tomorrow I'll leave much earlier for the ferry and go to Ithaca."

"You have to eat dinner. Will you dine with me this evening?"

She tried not to look at him or she'd get lost in those penetrating black eyes. "You've done more than enough for me when you've already missed your board meeting. I'm very grateful to you for coming to my rescue, but I refuse to take up any more of your time."

Zoe started to reach for her purse when he said, "Would you mind if I came by in the morning and drove you to the ferry?"

Her eyes flew to his in surprise. "Why would you do that?"

"Because I prevented you from leaving the taxi at the scene of the accident this morning. I made you too late to reach the port in time. It's the least I can do."

She shook her head. "I'm already in your debt for the fabulous lunch."

"I promise I'll get you there on time."

The man couldn't be dissuaded, and he'd been wonderful to her. *You know you want to see him again, Zoe.* After her divorce, she'd been leery about getting close to a man again, especially one so breathtaking.

"What about your work?"

"It's always there waiting. I'll meet you here

in front at seven thirty in the morning. How does that sound?"

The accident must have done something to her psyche because a part of her wanted to say yes to this gorgeous man who was little more than a stranger to her. But another part of her feared it wouldn't be wise. She clutched her purse. Once before in her life she'd made the mistake of being charmed by an attractive man with disastrous results.

"That's a very generous offer. Thank you for everything, but I really don't want to put you out."

"You won't. If you aren't here when I come by in the morning, then I'll accept that's your answer and you'll never see me again."

He opened the door for her so she could get out of the car. Without looking back, she hurried toward her flat located around the side of the building hidden behind a big tree. Much as she wanted to tell him she'd love a ride with him, she didn't dare.

* * *

Andreas watched the dark blond American beauty with the stunning figure run from him before he told the driver to head for the office. He couldn't remember anything like this happening to him before.

When Andreas had looked inside the damaged taxi earlier, his gaze had fused with a pair of azure-blue eyes so alive and brilliant, he'd been mesmerized.

He'd assumed she was in her early twenties. It totally surprised him when he learned she was a professor of the early nineteenth-century romance writers at UCLA in California, which meant she was older than he'd supposed.

He'd been instantly attracted to her in a way he couldn't explain. The woman's concern over the taxi driver had touched him. As for her keen intellect and interest in Lord Byron, he was intrigued. She didn't know it yet, but the two of them had a lot to talk about. He found himself planning a way to spend more time with her.

After the emotional turmoil he'd been in for

so long he didn't want to think about it, he was utterly shocked that he wanted to pursue this woman. But instinct told him that if she'd been put off by him, she wouldn't have walked with him to the limo after the accident, or have gone to lunch with him. Still, something else had held her back from accepting a ride from him to the ferry tomorrow.

He thought about the situation until he went to bed. If he was wrong and she didn't feel any sort of attraction to him, there was only one way to find out.

When morning came, he dressed in sport clothes and parked his car in front of her apartment at seven fifteen. For all he knew, she could have already left or changed her mind and done something else. If there was no sign of her, he'd told her he would let it go. But he knew he wouldn't like it.

At twenty-five after, a taxi pulled up behind him, letting him know she had no intention of going with him. Instead of leaving before she came out, Andreas wanted her to know he'd kept his word. He got out of his car and lounged against the passenger door to wait.

A few minutes later she walked out dressed in white cargo pants and a blue-and-white-print blouse with three-quarter sleeves. The sun streaks in her neck-length hair shone in the morning light. He couldn't look anywhere else before straightening. It diverted her attention.

The surprise in her blue eyes above those exquisite high cheekbones was 100 percent genuine. *"You!"* She hadn't thought he'd come.

"Good morning, *kyria*. I told you I would be here. I meant what I said. I'd like to take you to the ferry to make up for yesterday, but the decision is yours."

She smoothed a strand of hair behind her ear. "The thing is, my taxi is already here."

That comment told him all he needed to know. "I'll take care of it."

He walked around to talk to the driver. "Thanks for coming," he said in Greek and paid him triple what she would have had to pay him to go to the dock.

The driver was all smiles and pulled out into traffic.

Andreas headed for his car and opened the door for her. She came closer. "Now I feel terrible. My debts to you are adding up."

It hit him that as long as she wanted to be with him, nothing else mattered. And she *did*, otherwise she would have said no thank you and climbed in that taxi.

"Let's not talk about debts and enjoy the drive." He helped her in the car and took off. "I'm aware that you know nothing about me, but I assure you I'm not in the habit of picking up women who've been in an accident or otherwise."

That brought a smile to her lips. "I'm not in the habit of being picked up by a man on his way to a board meeting."

"Touché. Now that we have that out of the way, I'd like you to know the truth about me. Two days ago I filed for divorce and have a son, Ari, who's fifteen months old. He's my life." *Even if he isn't my birth son.* "But he's with his mother right now in Athens. They're living with her parents for the time being."

She turned to look at him. "I'm so sorry. I've been through a divorce and know how painful it is, but there were no children involved. The emptiness has to be unbearable."

He darted her a glance. She'd already been married…

"Life has a way of throwing us curves we never expected, like your accident yesterday. Right now I'm trying to make sense of everything. Believe it or not, doing something for you is helping."

She stirred in the seat. "What you've told me explains why you didn't care if you missed your board meeting."

"You're right about that. I'm trying to keep it together, but I couldn't go to work today, or stay at the villa. Thank you for helping me keep my sanity, *kyria*. You're just the company I need."

"I've been where you've been," she said compassionately. "If you'd like a job, why don't you come to Ithaca with me for the day? I could use an interpreter of your caliber."

"What caliber is that?"

"I asked my landlord about you. He said you're a very important man."

"Don't believe him."

She chuckled softly. "I knew it when the police officer recognized you and immediately acceded to your wishes."

The fact that she'd asked him to go to Ithaca with her had lifted his mood. They reached the dock and got in line to board the ferry. The four-hour trip across and back meant they wouldn't be home until eight or later.

Once they could leave the car, they went to the dining room to eat, then walked out on deck. "It's hard to believe this view is real," she murmured. "The green of the Ionian islands bathed by crystal blue waters is out of this world."

He'd never been around anyone as appreciative of everything as she was. As he'd told her earlier, she was easy to be with. "I couldn't agree more. Tell me why Ithaca is so important."

"When Lord Byron left Genoa in July of 1823, he traveled on a ship called the *Hercules* with Pietro Gamba and William Fletcher among others. They arrived at Cephalonia in August and made an expedition to Ithaca. He was filled with inspiration and did a lot of writing during that period. I want to visit the two museums in Vathy and see what memorabilia is there."

Being with Zoe made the time pass quickly. Soon they were able to drive onto the island and tour some of the archaeological sites before stopping at the museums.

"Tell me what those words say, Andreas." It was the first time she'd used his name. He enjoyed translating some of the lines from the marble commemorative stele of Byron for her.

"If this island belonged to me, I would bury all my books here and never go away," he told her.

"That's an interesting thing to say. He really was taken with the history of this place." She recorded Andreas's words in the notebook she carried in her purse. They worked well together and he regretted it when they had to leave to drive back to the ferry.

Again they ate aboard ship and discussed Ulysses, who was said to have been born on Ithaca or Cephalonia. She was so knowledge-able about literature in general, it was fascinat-ing to be with her.

When they got back to the apartment, he turned to her and told her his plans. "Tomor-row I'm leaving for Athens to be with my son. Temporary visitation has been worked out with the judge. I'm with him for two days, usually over the weekend. Then his mother has him for five and we go back and forth. It's unequal, but works for now because of my business sched-ule."

"You can't bring him here?"

"I could, but it's a lot of flying. Do you mind if I call you after I'm back?"

"Not at all, but just so you know, I'm leav-ing tomorrow to join my friends on holiday in Switzerland."

The news stunned him. He'd just met her and

already she was going away? "How long will you be gone?"

"I'm not sure." She reached for the door handle. "But I can't thank you enough for taking me to Ithaca today. It was a real treat, and I know you can't wait until tomorrow when you see your son. Have a safe trip, Andreas."

"Wait—let's exchange phone numbers so we can stay in touch."

"All right."

By then she'd already gotten out of the car. It was still light out. "Don't get in any accidents on your way home," she teased before disappearing around the big tree.

Andreas sat there for a few minutes, upset that he might not see her again. Before he pulled away, he phoned her.

She sounded breathless when she answered. "Andreas?"

"Hi. Just wanted to make sure I could reach you."

"You must have driven your mother crazy."

"Probably," he quipped. "Enjoy your trip."

"You, too."

He hung up and headed for the villa. Though he was counting the hours until he could be with Ari, there was someone else he'd be thinking about this weekend. Since he'd told her he was divorced with a son, she'd relaxed around him, like she might around a friend.

But he would never be able to think of her in the friend sense. She'd grown on him like mad today and belonged in an entirely different category. The thought of not seeing her again disturbed him a great deal.

CHAPTER TWO

WHEN ZOE'S PLANS with the girls didn't turn out, she flew back to Patras four days later and returned to her apartment in time to go to bed. Their long-awaited vacation in Switzerland had gone up in smoke.

Abby had fallen for a Burgundian vintner and had gone to France with him. Ginger had wanted to stay in Venice. Zoe had the idea she'd met a man because something was definitely keeping her there.

As for Zoe, she was excited to return to Greece. All the way back on the plane she debated whether to phone Andreas when she got there and let him know her plans had changed. But by the time she got ready for bed, she'd talked herself out of calling him.

Zoe had been a fool to ask him to go to

Ithaca with her and should forget him. What she needed to do was finish her Greek research and go home to California.

Once she got in bed and turned out the light, her phone rang. Was it Abby or Ginger? She shot up in bed and reached for her cell on the bedside table.

It was Andreas.

"Hello?" Her voice had a pathetic tremor.

"Zoe—I'm back from Athens and couldn't go to bed until I'd spoken with you. Are you enjoying your trip with your friends? Where are you?"

Hearing his deep familiar voice, she pressed a hand to her heart. "We had a lovely time, but circumstances changed and I'm actually back in Patras."

"You're here?" She could hear the excitement in his voice. It matched hers.

"Yes. How's your son?"

"I loved being with him, but tell me, what are your plans now?"

"Tomorrow I'm going to Ioannina."

"In that case I have an idea. I'll come by in the morning and drive us both there. Then we can talk."

"I can't let you do that. You have a company to run."

"Before you say no, hear me out. I'll take my laptop and work while you do your thing. There are several charming places to stay the night. I can call ahead for reservations."

"Andreas—stop. It isn't fair to you."

"Why not? I thought you understood you're helping me. I'm not ready to be imprisoned in my office yet. Do you know what I mean?"

"I'm afraid I do," she answered quietly. "Of course I'd love to drive with you, but if you change your mind and something unexpected comes up, please don't worry about me."

"Thank you for saying yes. Now I can sleep. See you tomorrow morning at eight thirty. Good night, *kyria*."

Zoe lay back against the pillow, excited for morning to come. At seven she awakened and hurried to wash her hair and get ready in a new skirt and top she'd bought recently.

When she walked outside, Andreas was there dressed in sport clothes, looking like her idea of a Greek god. His black eyes traveled over her.

"It's good to see you again," he told her.

"I'm happy to see you, too. I wasn't sure I'd be back again and will have to tell you what happened. But first I want to hear about Ari."

He helped her in his car and they left the city, traveling northwest. Zoe found herself enchanted by the city of Ioannina, spread out around Lake Pamvotida. The wealthy, aristocratic city, two hours northwest of Patras, included the cultures of Christianity, Islam and Judaism. The variety of its shops and food depicted the traditions.

After spending part of the day in the library where she did research, Andreas took her to a traditional coffeehouse where they were served sugar pie and an alcohol-free liqueur. He explained it was a mixture of organic vinegar, nectar, fruit syrups and herbs, drunk with crushed ice.

"It tastes like it must have alcohol in it. I love this drink. I wonder if Lord Byron drank it, but so far I haven't come across it in my research."

Andreas chuckled. "You have no idea how much fun you are to be with. Why is Ioannina so important to your research?"

"Byron wrote part of *Childe Harold's Pilgrimage* here."

"I've read some of it. His wish for man to be free touches me most."

She took a deep breath. "He said the most profound things. When I read his writings, I feel like I'm in touch with the divine. This is the essence of what Magda hopes will be conveyed by her film."

"How can she fail with someone like you supplying the inspiration?"

The tone in his voice found its way into her heart. "You're nice to listen to me. What can I do for you?"

"Let's talk a walk along the lake back to our hotel. Later we'll get dinner."

He'd found them a small, adorable hideaway at the water's edge she'd loved on sight. Zoe had never experienced a day like this before. Since meeting him in such an unorthodox way, she was discovering Greece all over again through the eyes of a native son.

Zoe couldn't help but be sorry for the breakup of his marriage. He hadn't offered an explanation and she didn't want one. All she knew was that he was an exceptional man and she felt lucky to know him. But even as she thought it, the memory of her bad marriage crept into her mind. She'd fallen for Nate too fast, too. She shook off the thought.

"Tell me about Ari. Was he thrilled to see you?"

A sweet smile broke out on his handsome features when he thought of his son. "He loves to play so hard, he wore me out."

"I'm sure it's painful to leave him."

"You can't imagine."

"But you only have to wait two more days until you see him again. We've already gotten you through today." He chuckled. "Why don't we buy some souvlaki at a kiosk along here and eat it on the terrace of the hotel. I don't want to go inside until we have to. The temperature here is heavenly."

His gaze played over her. "You're reading my mind."

After he bought their food, they reached the hotel and sat down at a table to watch the sun go down. Another couple had come out on the patio involved in each other. The lovers couldn't have found a more romantic place.

Glancing at them, an ache started up in Zoe's heart. What would it be like to come here with the man you loved? One who loved you? A man like Andreas…

The second the thought came into her mind, she realized she'd made a mistake to let him drive her here. Of course there was no question of their getting involved romantically. They were simply acquaintances who'd met under unusual circumstances, but she'd be crazy to spend any more time with him.

He'd barely separated from his wife and clearly longed for his son. It was already June. She'd be going back to California soon. The old adage about ships passing in the night couldn't have been more apropos.

All these months she'd been in Greece doing her job, not needing anyone, least of all a man. The taxi accident had brought them together, but for this to go on was ridiculous.

Already he was coloring her world in ways she didn't want. She needed to stop this foolishness before she got too used to his being with her. Thank goodness he couldn't afford to stay away from his work any longer.

"Andreas? That tasted good, but now I need to go in and write up some notes before I get too tired. I hope you don't mind if I turn in."

She heard him take a deep breath. "I'll walk you to your room."

"That won't be necessary."

"I brought you here and want you to be safe."

Zoe was surprised by the firm tone of his voice. But he was a caring, thoughtful man and would be like this in any situation.

They headed to her room in the east wing of the hotel. She knew his was in the other wing. He waited while she opened the door.

Zoe went inside and peeked around at him. "Maybe we can get breakfast en route back to Patras."

One black brow lifted. "You're through with your research here?"

"I'm sure."

"What's your next destination?"

"I don't know yet. Ever since I came to Greece, I've constantly sent out emails to various places for information. The answers come back if there's something I need to research. I'll know tomorrow when I receive more responses. Good night, Andreas."

"Good night," he whispered.

As he turned away, she shut the door. Her explanation had been the right thing to say. If she'd told him what her destination would be tomorrow, she knew in her heart he'd tell her he'd drive her there.

While he was dealing with this huge change in his life—something Zoe knew all about after divorcing her husband for his infidelity—she realized this time with Andreas was a distraction that was helping him to cope with what he was going through. But she couldn't afford to keep it up. It was far too risky to her own peace of mind.

They reached Patras at 11:30 a.m., when he pulled the car up in front of her apartment. He'd taken Zoe to see the monastery in Varlaam on the way back. Afterward they'd enjoyed breakfast at the quaint Taverna Gardenia in one of the narrow passageways.

"What a treat to have gone there! I suppose you've climbed those one hundred and ninety-five steps to the top before?" she teased.

"Guilty."

"It would take someone a lot more courageous than me to do it."

He smiled at the inexhaustible, breathtaking woman standing on the sidewalk while he retrieved her small suitcase from the car. Zoe didn't fool him. She'd been in Greece on her own since January, digging up material in out-of-the-way places, talking to strangers, taking risks. She embraced adventure.

"I'll call you later."

Her eyes flashed blue fire. "From *work*, I hope. I've kept you from it too long."

"It's been the best medicine I could have asked for."

"I'm glad. And just think? After today you only have to wait one more day before you sweep your little boy into your arms again."

She understood him like no one else. "Speaking of Ari, I never did show you a picture of him." He pulled out his phone and scrolled to his photo gallery. "I bought him a little pair of sunglasses."

Zoe took the phone from him and broke into an infectious smile after studying it. "He's absolutely adorable. I don't know how you stand the separation." She handed it back to him.

He put his cell in his shirt pocket. "We do what we have to do."

"Isn't that the truth. I won't tell you to have a wonderful day, but hope it will be all right if I wish you a *productive* one? Then my guilt won't be so bad."

Andreas burst into laughter. He never knew what she was going to say next. But she was right. He'd played hooky from work for long enough. "I've enjoyed our time together."

"So have I," she came right back. "Now I need to get going." She picked up her case and started toward her flat. Before she rounded the tree, she waved at him.

He got back in his car and headed for work. His personal assistant probably couldn't wait to show him the mountain of decisions to make and contracts to look over, but he didn't care. Being with Zoe Perkins had given him a new lease on life.

The next time he lifted his head was around

five thirty when he reached for his phone to call Zoe. He was getting hungry and wanted to take her to dinner. To his satisfaction she answered on the second ring.

"Andreas—" She sounded vibrant. "How did you survive your first day back?"

"More to the point, what about you? Where are you? How soon can I pick you up? I'm starving."

"So am I, but I'm actually on my way to dinner with a group of professors here in Prevesa."

The news came as a blow. His black brows knit together. "That's three hours away by car. How come you didn't say anything this morning?"

"I didn't know until I looked at my emails."

Andreas needed to calm down. "How did you get there?"

"I rented a car because I knew I'd need to drive around a lot once I got here. I'm really lucky because these people have fresh information for me about Lord Byron. This is like finding gold at the end of the rainbow. I'll probably be here three or four days."

The wind went right out of his sails. "That means I won't be able to see you until I get back again from Athens."

"I should be in Patras by then—or shortly after. Thanks for calling me. Have fun with Ari."

That was a given, but as for anything else, he felt like his lifeline had been cut during his space walk and he was cast into the void. "I hope this trip brings big results for you. Talk to you soon."

He hung up and left the office for his grandparents' villa. They'd been devastated by the news about his filing for a separation, but understood how Lia's painful betrayal had brought about the end of their marriage.

Not only that, it had upset his grandfather that he hadn't been at the board meeting the day of the taxi accident. Andreas needed to reassure them on all counts that everything was all right.

But the truth was, he couldn't bear to go home until he was ready to collapse in bed.

When the time came to fly to Athens, he was more than ready to enjoy his son. Ari was the joy of his life and they had a marvelous two days and nights together. The only way he could stand to leave him this time was hoping that Zoe would be there when he got back to Patras.

After his jet landed and he headed for his villa, he phoned Zoe. It would be the first time they'd spoken since he'd talked to her the day she'd gone to Prevesa. Andreas wasn't known for his patience, but in her case he didn't want to crowd her while she was doing her work.

This time she didn't answer until the fourth ring. "Good morning, Kyrie Gavras." She'd never called him that before. "Are you back in Patras? How was your visit with Ari?"

"I just flew in and my time with my son was wonderful as usual. I want to know about you."

"As I told you before, I found a treasure trove here."

He had trouble swallowing. "So you're still in Prevesa?"

"Not exactly. One of the literature professors from Turkey invited me to return to Anatalya with him. I'll be here for two weeks, maybe less, then I'll be back in Patras. He's an expert on Lord Byron and has incredible information with a fresh perspective. We'll be traveling to Bodrum and Ephesus, where there are other scholars he wants me to meet. He's very excited about the film Magda is making."

Andreas was listening, but he also imagined the professor was particularly excited about being around anyone as beautiful and vivacious as Zoe.

His eyes closed tightly. "I'm glad you're finding new information."

"It's fantastic." She sounded happy.

"The best of luck to you, Zoe."

"Thank you so much. I'll call you when I know my flight from Anatalya."

"Why don't I pick you up at the airport?"

"That would be lovely, but only if it's convenient for you."

"I'll make it convenient."

She laughed. He'd missed that sound, he'd missed her more than he could believe. "Bye for now."

Zoe's heart almost palpitated out of her chest when she saw Andreas with his black hair and burning black eyes standing at the luggage pickup waiting for her. He'd dressed in one of his elegant silk suits, this time a gray one with a dazzling white shirt and tie. The man was bigger than life and so sinfully handsome, it was shocking to her.

She'd hoped to get some perspective while she'd been away from him, but instead the opposite had happened. Her bad experience with Nate hadn't seemed to have taught her anything. The ache in her heart had grown more serious while she'd been away from Andreas. Seeing him again had turned it into real pain.

His gaze played over her in that way only

he could do, causing her insides to melt on the spot. "The world traveler is back home. How does it feel?"

Like I'm going to die from happiness.

"I'm glad to be back, but it's not going to be for long." Let him know now.

The gleam in his eyes vanished. "What's next on your agenda?"

"Since I uncovered new information while I was in Turkey, I have to go back to Messolonghi tomorrow for a week."

"Do you have time to eat lunch with me before you're off again?"

"I'd love it." She reached for her suitcase, but he took it from her.

"My car is out in the short-term parking. Let's go." They walked out together. After he helped her in the car and got behind the wheel, he said, "Do you want to go to your apartment first?"

"Oh, no. I don't want to put you out. We can eat on the way in. You pick a place."

"What are you in the mood for?"

"Anything. You can't get a bad meal in Greece."

He started the car and drove away. "As opposed to Turkey?"

"The food there was delicious, but you know what I mean. I've been here since January and have loved it all."

"That's nice to hear." He drove them to a restaurant where the specialty was moussaka with a béchamel sauce he liked. They could eat outside on the patio and enjoy some house wine.

The waiter took their order. When he walked away, she smiled at Andreas. "How is Ari? Do you have any more pictures to show me?"

"As a matter of fact, I do." He pulled out his phone and they laughed over the photos for a few minutes until their meal came. They were both hungry. Then he changed the subject.

"Will you let me drive you to Messolonghi? We could leave later today and enjoy an evening together there."

"You're so generous to me, but this afternoon I have an appointment at the University of Patras with a professor who's finally back from his vacation. He has some vital information for me."

"How were you planning to get there?"

"Call for a taxi."

His dark eyes narrowed on her face. "Do you dare?"

The question made her chuckle. "If *you're* offering to drive me, I won't say no. But I'll be there for at least two hours."

"Then I'll do some errands and come back for you. If you want to go back to the apartment, I'll drive you and then we'll leave for Messolonghi."

Zoe realized she couldn't say no to him. He was determined to spend time with her, and heaven help her, she was so thrilled to be with him she could hardly stand it.

They ate dessert before he took her to the university. She waved him off before hurrying inside. Zoe didn't think the dean of the literature department had summoned her because his information was new, but she was curious.

What really stunned her was that he'd been talking to others in the humanities department and was offering her a temporary post to teach there in their theater department for the fall semester. Byron had written a series of plays she could teach in a curriculum she'd developed.

The earlier mention of her association with Magda Collier had no doubt excited them to the point they'd made this offer. But as tempting and alluring as it was because it would keep her in Andreas's sphere, she turned it down. No way did she dare accept.

When she'd met Nate, she'd fallen for him too fast and had rushed into a serious relationship with him with disastrous results. If she stayed in Greece and was given this position at the university, it would be throwing her into temptation's way with Andreas. She had to keep reminding herself that she'd be leaving Greece soon and had no intention of coming back.

After telling the dean she was honored and flattered to have been considered, but couldn't accept the offer, she left his office and waited outside in front of the building enjoying the view until Andreas came for her.

They drove into town. Once he'd dropped her off at the apartment long enough to pack fresh clothes, she got back in his car and they left for Messolonghi.

She'd spent time there earlier in the year. It was the place where the Greek rebels fought in the Greek War of Independence against the Ottoman Empire. It was there that Byron came to join Greece in its fight for freedom.

"Refresh my memory about that last day," Andreas asked her.

"From what I know, Byron rode his horse by the waters of the lagoon, then to the Chapel of the Virgin by the Palm Tree, and then for many more miles onto Aetolicon. On that fateful day he was caught in the downpour of a storm and returned completely soaked to the home in Messolonghi where he was staying. That's when the sweating and fever started. He became seriously ill and died at the age of thirty-six."

He shot her glance. "What more do you expect to learn about that day by going there?"

"I'm curious to compare some facts with the Turkish accounts I've just gathered."

Andreas shook his head. "Does that mind of yours ever turn off?"

She flashed him a radiant smile. "I hope not."

After they reached Messolonghi, Zoe had booked a local hotel. After she'd checked in, Andreas walked her through the Garden of Heroes where Lord Byron was featured. According to his will, his heart was buried there beneath the statue and his body shipped back to England.

As she'd walked with Andreas, she knew she'd come close to losing her own heart. But it had happened so quickly! How could she be feeling this way after her last painful experience? Zoe was at the point where she didn't trust her own judgment and was feeling so vulnerable, she was frightened.

Because you know that what you feel for Andreas is more than what you've ever felt for anyone before.

They had a meal of superb grilled eel at a

nearby café. He was definitely a fish man, but this would be their last dinner together.

Zoe looked at her watch. "It's getting late, Andreas. Don't you think you'd better get back to Patras if you're expecting to fly to Athens in the morning?"

"It's only an hour's drive. Why do I get the feeling you're trying to get rid of me?"

She sucked in her breath. "That's the first cruel thing you've ever said to me. I thought we were friends."

"I'm sorry if it came off sounding that way."

"I'm the one who's sorry. I guess I worry that you're a man with so many responsibilities. You've done everything for me since that accident."

"It's obvious that you're not used to letting anyone help you."

That was a plain fact. "You're right. I need to learn to be more gracious. Thank you for this whole day and the dinner tonight."

"You're welcome. If you're ready, I'll walk

you to the hotel and say goodbye for another week."

Another seven days away from him. How would she be able to handle it?

He accompanied her as far as the hotel foyer. "I plan to come for you when you're through here. I'll call you."

"I know you can't wait for tomorrow to see Ari. It makes me happy just thinking about the two of you together."

"Good luck with your research."

They were talking around each other. She could see a little nerve throbbing at the corner of his mouth before he turned on his heel and walked out of the hotel.

Zoe hurried up to her room on the second floor and burst into tears. This had to end.

For the rest of the week she did as much research as she could. On the sixth day, she packed up and rented a car to drive back to Patras. From there she made a plane reservation for a night flight to Venice. For the rest of the day she got her laundry and packing done.

She couldn't stay in Greece any longer. Zoe had been the first woman Andreas had turned to since filing for his separation. It was possible he and Lia might even reconcile given a little more time and no outside distractions. He'd told Zoe that Lia still wanted him back. Zoe didn't doubt it and couldn't help but wonder if that knowledge didn't work on Andreas. If he wanted to try again with Lia, Zoe knew it would kill her.

Even if that didn't happen, in time there would be more women when Andreas was finally free. Nate had found another woman before they were ever divorced. It was inevitable the same thing would happen with Andreas. Zoe wasn't the kind of a woman to hold a man like him for long, not after she couldn't keep even Nate interested.

No matter where they went, every female eye followed Andreas because of his looks and sheer charisma. Her legs went weak whenever she saw him waiting out in front of her apartment.

Here she was at twenty-six, on the verge of

being swept away by the sheer male beauty and magnetism of Andreas Gavras. She'd learned he was the renowned hotelier of Gavras House Properties and an influential, fabulously wealthy business tycoon from the powerful Gavras family. Their name figured heavily in the economic future of western Greece.

Though she was madly attracted to him, she had to get away while she still could. It would be impossible to go on remaining just friends with him, not when deep down she wanted him in all the ways a woman wanted a man. And when his interest turned to someone else, then what?

After paying the bill, she left at eight that evening and sat in the airport waiting for the call to board her flight. That's when her phone rang. She checked the caller ID. A moan escaped when she saw Andreas's name. With a pounding heart, she clicked on. This was it.

"Andreas? How are you?"

"Looking forward to seeing you. It's good to hear your voice. I thought I'd better call now to find out how soon you'll be ready in the morning."

She started to tremble. "I'm so glad you called when you did. I have something important to tell you."

There was a definite pause before he said, "Does this mean you need to stay there longer?"

"No. I just received news from my two friends. They're both in Venice right now and are begging me to come. One of them, Ginger, is being married to a Venetian on July 5, which is in less than a week. The three of us want to spend some time together before the wedding, so I'm on my way there now."

"What do you mean you're on your way?" His voice sounded fierce.

She gripped her phone tighter. "I'm at the airport and they're calling for my flight right now. I have to go."

"When will you be coming back?"

Heaven help me.

"I'm flying straight back to California after I leave Venice. I've been away a long time and need to get my affairs in order before I start teaching again this fall."

"You can't leave yet. There are things you don't know. Things I need to tell you."

"Andreas—I'm so sorry. I have to board the plane. But let me say this one last thing. You'll never know what meeting you has meant to me. I'll always be grateful to you for everything. You're the finest man I've ever known. I guarantee that in time your life is going to be happy again. Take care, my good friend."

CHAPTER THREE

ZOE STOOD NEXT to Abby and her husband, Raoul Decorvet, in front of the fabulous Palazzo Della Scala in Venice. Together with the other wedding guests, they watched Vittorio kiss a radiant Ginger before helping her climb in the flower-laden gondola in their wedding finery.

Off on a honeymoon and a heavenly future, and Zoe couldn't have been happier for her, or for Abby, who'd also recently married her titled Frenchman and now lived in Burgundy.

Abby and Raoul had invited Zoe to stay with them until she had to fly back to California. That was her plan. But later in the day when she went up to the guest room in the palazzo, she ended up calling her friend.

"Abby? There's something I have to tell you. If you can't talk now—"

"Raoul is still downstairs with Vittorio's family discussing the lawsuit being waged against him. What's wrong?"

Zoe broke down and told her about Andreas. "Do you think I'm crazy to want to go back when nothing can come of it?"

"You're asking *me* a question like that? The woman who left for France with a virtual stranger who might or might not have been on the level about showing me a poem of Lord Byron's?"

She laughed through the tears. "But Raoul wasn't just working his way through a troubled separation. I don't know any details about Andreas's marriage and don't want to, but I've seen the pain in his eyes. Sometimes he seems miles away. Whatever he's holding back, he hasn't shared it with me. I can't handle it."

"At least this Andreas told you up front he was separated from his wife and had a child, but it sounds like he's being careful. I'm sorry you left before he could explain more. It might have been important."

Zoe wiped the moisture off her cheeks. "I don't know, but it doesn't really matter because I'm afraid to get in any deeper. Like Nate, he's no more ready for a lasting relationship than a fly. That's the only kind I want and probably won't ever experience. I've been through one divorce and have no desire to be used or hurt because he's looking for temporary comfort."

"It doesn't sound like he's using you, Zoe. Quite the opposite, in fact, considering his attention to you and the help he's given you."

"I'll admit he's been incredible."

"That's honest at least," Abby murmured. "Look—I hear what you're saying, but I can tell you're really torn up at leaving him. I never thought I'd see you in this condition. Driving off into the sunset with Raoul after what Nigel did to me was close to lunacy, except that I felt something for him I had to explore. Now look what's happened!"

"Your story is like a fairy tale."

"Ginger's is, too. She'd adored her husband who'd died and thought she could never find that happiness again. Then she met Vittorio, who won her heart. Now she's the wife of a fantastic, important Venetian. Maybe it's your turn."

My turn for more regrets.

"Much as I'd selfishly hoped you would stay at the chateau with me for the rest of the summer, my advice is to go back and hear him out."

She sucked in her breath. "Abby? I can't believe you're telling me this. Do you remember the conversation the three of us had at the vineyard in Geneva at the start of our vacation? When you told us about the French Realtor you'd met, Ginger and I were fearful for you. Something that sounded so good couldn't possibly be true."

"But it was, Zoe, even though he turned out not to be a Realtor."

"I know," she whispered.

"What could it hurt to see him one more time and hear what he has to say? You were pretty abrupt to cut it off on the phone with him when he had no idea you'd been planning to leave. It isn't as if he did something you couldn't abide. Or did he?"

"Of course not. If anything—"

"He hasn't even kissed you?" Abby broke in on her.

Her face went hot. "I told you. It hasn't been that kind of a relationship. I don't know what you'd call it."

"Then go back and find out. If I'm wrong and seeing him again only causes you more pain and frustration, then come to Burgundy. My invitation is always open. As for tomorrow, on our way home Raoul and I will drive you to the airport in the morning, if that's what you want."

Zoe's hand squeezed the phone tightly. "I'm afraid it *is* what I want. You're the greatest friend in the world, Abby."

After they hung up, she booked a flight to Patras. Abby had given her the courage. She needed to see Andreas again one last time and tell him the truth. That she'd started to develop feelings for him but it was wrong to act on them while he still wasn't free.

* * *

Andreas stared gloomily out the window of his private jet as it headed to Patras airport from Athens, where he'd spent a couple of days on business. After Zoe had said goodbye to him a week ago, he'd almost gone out of his mind. Ari was the only constant in his life and he didn't see enough of him. Knowing Zoe was on her way to California was killing him.

When he wasn't with Ari at Gavras House in Athens, Andreas wanted to spend every free minute with Zoe. He'd thought she'd felt the same way until that phone call. Her goodbye had gutted him. He'd experienced a staggering sense of loss and asked her to listen to him, but she'd hung up. He hadn't had the opportunity to tell her what was on his mind.

The next time he went to Athens, he'd had plans to take her with him so she could meet Ari. Ever since he'd met her, Andreas had sensed something earthshaking was happening to him and she was the reason.

Whatever had frightened her off, he vowed

this wasn't going to be the end. He knew where to find her, even if it meant flying to California.

All these thoughts and more bombarded him as the jet landed and he got in the back of the limousine. He told his driver to take him to the Gavras building complex in the city center. His office manager, Lukas, needed his signature on new construction contracts that would take time to study.

When he walked into his inner sanctum, Lukas followed him inside. "Welcome back. Before we get started, I received a phone call from a woman who is most anxious to talk to you. The number is on your desk."

"Was she calling from Yorgos Zika's office?" He supposed it was something to do with Lia asking for more money to finalize the purchase of the Athenian villa she'd chosen. He would pay it. The sooner she was settled, the sooner he would change the temporary terms of visitation.

"No. This woman is an American and asked to speak to you if you were available."

His heart hammered wildly. *Zoe?* Why did

she call his office instead of reaching him on his cell phone? Was she still in Italy? Andreas was incredulous.

"What did you tell her?"

"That you were flying in from Athens sometime today."

"Thank you, Lukas. I'll make the call, then we'll go over the contracts."

He nodded and left, shutting the door.

Andreas sat down at his desk and called her cell phone. When he heard her say hello, she sounded as breathless as he felt.

"Zoe?"

"Andreas—I wasn't sure you would bother to return my call. In fact I—I can't believe you did." Her voice faltered.

Excitement swept through him. "Why didn't you call my cell?"

"I was afraid you might not answer it if you knew it was me on the other end. I hoped you'd at least pick up if you were at your office."

He shook his head at her logic. "Where are you?"

"In Patras at my same apartment."

Patras? His pulse raced off the charts. "I thought you were in Italy, or had flown on to California."

"I did attend the wedding, but then I flew back here this morning…because I owe you an apology."

Maybe he was dreaming. "What do you mean?"

"The way I left Greece so abruptly, I was afraid I might have offended you. Ever since we met, you've been nothing but kind to me. When I look back on the time we managed to spend together in spite of our busy schedules, you were always the one giving me rides, taking care of me, paying for our food."

"It was my pleasure from the very beginning. You know that."

"But it was very rude and inconsiderate of me to announce that I was leaving without hearing what you had to say. I just want you to know that no researcher from America who'd never been to Greece until now could have been so blessed as to have you of all people for a guide, translator and friend."

Her touching words caused his throat to swell. "We met at a dark time for me. The last few weeks with you have been my salvation." She could have no idea.

"And mine. Magda Collier was ecstatic over the research I sent to the script writers, and you had something to do with that."

"I couldn't be happier for you."

"To show my gratitude for all you did for me, could I take you to dinner this evening if you're free? My treat? Magda paid me well so my funds have been replenished."

His eyes closed tightly. He'd already made arrangements to eat dinner with his grandparents at their villa and give his grandfather another business update. But this night with Zoe was too important. Andreas would drop by to see them and explain before going home to get ready.

"I'd be honored."

"I thought we'd go to Naut-oiko. When I visited the University of Patras, the dean told me it's the best seafood restaurant around."

There was a lot that went on inside her he still had to find out.

"The dean was right. What makes it even more perfect is that it's right on the sea. We can take a stroll along the beach after. What time shall I come by for you?" His watch said four fifteen.

"Would seven work for you?"

Andreas wasn't sure he could wait that long to see her again. "I'll be out in front."

"I'll look for you."

He hung up a new man who didn't have time to look over contracts today. With his adrenaline surging, he left the office for his car, telling Lukas he'd work on them early in the morning instead.

Zoe changed her mind three times before deciding on a floral print of pink, purple and coral on a white dress with a round neck and cap sleeves. If they were going to walk along the shore in the ninety-degree heat, the fluttery material was summery and light. She'd never worn it with Andreas. Everywhere they went, people recognized him. Tonight at dinner she wanted to look her best.

She hadn't known what kind of greeting she'd get when he'd returned her call. The minute she'd heard his deep enticing voice, she'd started talking way too fast and hadn't given him a second to breathe. Zoe almost fainted when he said he'd be honored to go to dinner with her.

While she washed and dried her hair, she thought about her conversation with Abby. What if she hadn't come back to see Andreas? Thank goodness she'd taken her friend's advice and had been able to tell him how much his friendship had meant to her. Running away from him the other day without allowing him to talk to her had been incredibly childish.

When she told him tonight that she'd be flying to Dijon tomorrow to stay with Abby and Raoul until she went back to California, she would feel she'd shown him the respect he deserved.

Today, while she'd had time after her arrival in Patras, she'd gone to a toy store and bought his son a set of three little ModMobiles on wheels, with interchangeable foam pieces. They were colorful and looked fun to play with. The clerk had put them in a gift bag.

Andreas, with his influence, had done things for her she could never repay. But she knew how much he adored his son and decided a gift for his little boy would please him.

Zoe brushed her hair into its usual windblown style and wore her floral enamel earrings. After applying a peach-scented lotion, she put on her favorite coral lipstick. Once she'd reached for her purse and the gift bag, she felt ready to walk out of the flat in her white leather sandals. It was only ten to seven, but her heart was pounding so hard, she couldn't stay inside any longer.

This evening she found him lounging against the passenger door of his silver Mercedes sedan with his arms folded. He'd come early, too. Though he looked sensational in everything he wore, the black silk shirt and khaki chinos covering his powerful legs made him more danger-ously attractive than ever before.

His penetrating black eyes roved over her, missing nothing. It made her think he was see-ing her for the first time. Zoe sensed a marked difference in him that caused her insides to flut-ter. This was a new Andreas, throwing her off balance.

He straightened to his full height and opened the door as she walked up to him, swallowing hard. "Andreas—thank you for letting me do something for you tonight, even if you had to pick me up."

One corner of his sensual mouth lifted. "Being a beach-city girl from California, your boss should have paid you enough money to buy the latest Porsche you once told me you coveted. Then you could have picked *me* up. I never saw anyone work harder than you."

She felt the sincerity of his unexpected com-pliment to her bones. "That's high praise com-ing from a man the media touts as the human dynamo of Greek industry."

Her arm brushed against his well-defined chest as she climbed in the car. The mere brief contact darted to every atom of her body. He walked around and got behind the wheel. She could smell the familiar faint scent of the lime soap he'd used in the shower. There wasn't anything about him that didn't bring her alive.

You're in such trouble, Zoe.

An excellent driver, he pulled into traffic and they headed for Rion, a suburb eight kilometers to the northeast of the city. It sat at the foot of Mount Panachaico. This evening she marveled over the view of the heavenly blue Gulf of Corinth spanned by the Rion-Antirion Bridge. The miracle of engineering linked the Peloponnese with mainland Greece.

Andreas had been right. She had a natural affinity for water and sunshine. How she adored Greece, the land of pristine beaches and twelve hours of daylight in summer! Tonight the sun wouldn't set until close to nine. To be here with him like this was better than any dream where he was always part of it, but forever out of reach and shrouded in mystery.

"Now that you've finally finished with your research, do you feel like a woman without a cause?"

She feared he could see right through her. "You're a very intuitive man and already know the answer."

They soon reached the delightful-looking open-air restaurant with large white umbrellas to shade the tables. He parked on the side of the road next to the beach and shut off the engine.

"Andreas? Before we get out, I wanted you to have this." She handed him the bag she'd kept on her lap.

He shot her a surprised glance. "Dinner *and* gifts? What have I done to deserve all this?"

"Take a peek."

In seconds he'd pulled out the box and opened it. The smile that broke out on his handsome face was worth everything. "Ari is going to love these."

"They look fun to me, too, and indestructible.

That photo you showed me of him in your sunglasses tickled me. I may not have met him, but I can just picture him pushing these around on the sand, pretending he's at one of your hotel construction sites. Your little boy is so lucky to have a great role model in his remarkable father."

She felt him hesitate before he said, "You're the one who's remarkable." Just now his deep voice sounded husky. Something had been going on in his mind she couldn't decipher. "So tell me the real reason you've come back."

The truth, Zoe.

"Since we met, I've developed feelings for you. Guilty feelings because you're not free. It frightened me and I ran away. That was childish. You deserved to know the truth face-to-face. If I've embarrassed you, I'm sorry."

He was quiet so long, she couldn't help but wonder what he was thinking. In a minute he gathered the toys into the bag and placed it on the back seat before getting out of the car to help her.

The restaurant was getting crowded, but she'd reserved a table that had an exquisite view of the gulf. The host showed them where to sit and the waiter came right over.

Zoe gave Andreas a brief look. "Please choose whatever you want and I'll have the same."

"You trust me?" he quipped.

"How can you ask me a question like that?"

With a subtle smile, he gave the order to the waiter. In a minute they were served Greek frappe known as iced coffee. "This is the ideal drink for a hot night. Try it."

She did his bidding. "This is delicious."

He put down his half-empty glass and sat forward. "Just so there's no question, I've developed feelings for you, too. In time I intend to act on them, but not yet. That's what I was anxious to tell you before you left for Venice."

Her heart could hardly take it.

"Since you've come back to Patras and we've established détente, would you be willing to tell me your plans now?"

She moistened her lips nervously. "Abby and

Raoul have invited me to spend some time at their vineyard until I need to return to America."

"Could you put that off for a while? I was hoping you'd consider flying to Athens with me the day after tomorrow. It's my time for visitation. I'd like you to meet Ari. If you went with me, you could give him that gift yourself."

A tiny gasp escaped. She was incredulous over what he'd just proposed. He wanted her to meet his son? Her heart thudded from anxiety and excitement all at once.

Abby had urged her to return to Patras and hear what Andreas had to say, but this was the last thing she'd expected. Before she could answer, the waiter returned to pour them some white wine. This was followed by plates of sizzling salmon filets and a side dish of mouthwatering fried mashed potatoes stuffed with *anthotyro* cheese and spinach.

"Does your silence mean you'd rather not postpone your plans to stay with your friends?" he asked after the waiter walked away.

She'd probably offended him again when it was the last thing she ever wanted to do. "It isn't that, Andreas. If I didn't say anything, it's because I'm so surprised at your suggestion."

He cocked his dark head. "I've wanted to take you before now, but I didn't want my plans to interfere with your work while you were finishing up your research. That's why it was a shock to me when you left Patras so abruptly. I hadn't realized that day had come and you were ready to move on."

Abby had been right about everything.

"Now you know why I left the way I did." She took a drink of wine. "Don't you think it might upset Ari if I'm with you?"

"If you'll come with me, we'll find out."

Andreas...

They both started to eat. "I'll arrange a room in the same hotel for you where I stay. There's a garden and a pond where he plays, not to mention the children's zoo and Happy Train."

"Is that the red one I saw on the streets of Athens?"

"Yes. It visits all the important places. Ari loves to ride on it. We'll be gone two days and nights. Is that something you'd like to do? If not, I'll be disappointed, but I'll understand."

When she'd finished all she could eat, she eyed him directly. "If you don't think Ari will be upset that you brought a visitor with you, then I'd be very happy to meet him."

He wiped his mouth with a napkin. "I'm glad you said that because there's something else I'd like to ask you. Tomorrow I must fly to Lakithra for the grand opening of our latest hotel. I won't have to be there long. How would you like to come with me? We'll have lunch at the hotel and test out the menu before we return to Patras."

She blinked. "You're talking about the village on Kefalonia?" He nodded. "Where I went to see the Rock of Byron?"

"The very one. The property for the hotel was in our family."

"You're kidding—"

"It's all true." His faint smile set her pulse racing. "The family decided to erect a hotel to honor Lord Byron and three of our ancestors living there who fought in the war for independence against the Turks."

"*That's* the reason you know so much about him. Do you have any old records?"

"If you're referring to diaries, no, otherwise I would have shown them to you. But our ancestors were part of the group funded by Lord Byron, who sold his estate in Scotland and raised twenty thousand pounds sterling toward that effort. We've named it Gavras House, Lakithra—Lord Byron."

She sat back. "What an absolutely fantastic thing for you to do!"

Andreas finished his wine. "When were you there?"

"In March."

"It would barely have been under construction then."

"You never mentioned a thing about it!"

One black brow lifted. "Knowing why you'd come to Greece, I'd hoped to surprise you when it was finished."

But she'd left Patras before he could tell her what he'd been hiding…

She shook her head. "You've surprised me, Andreas Gavras! I'd love to go!" Her cry coincided with the arrival of their white chocolate panna cotta dessert.

Before the waiter walked away, she said, "When you're ready to bring us the bill, please give it to me."

He darted Andreas a glance before glancing back at her. "Very good, *kyria*."

"The waiter knows who you are," she said after he'd walked away.

"If that's true, then he's thinking what a lucky man I am to be wined and dined by the most beautiful woman in Greece."

Zoe smiled. "Quoting Charlotte Bronte from the pen of Jane Eyre. 'Decidedly, you, sir, have had too much wine.'" She'd taken liberties with the quote. "But I'd be a fool not to enjoy the flattery. In the words of Lord Byron, 'Sermons and soda can come later.'"

His eyes lingered on her mouth, sending shivers through her. "Do your college students know how lucky they are to have you for their teacher?"

Everything Andreas said and did was getting to her. Thank goodness the waiter came back so she could pay him in cash and leave a big tip. "The dinner was excellent."

"Efkaristo, kyria."

Andreas stood up and collected her. "Shall we go get our feet wet?"

"That's a good idea. Maybe we won't need the sermons and soda after all to clear our heads."

He walked her back to the car, where she put her bag on the floor and they removed their shoes. After locking it, he reached for her hand and held it as they headed toward the water. Could there be a more romantic spot anywhere on earth? The sun had slipped below the horizon of this magical evening. To her mind, Greece was a land for lovers and Andreas was the most gorgeous man alive.

"You're not still frightened of me, are you?"

The unexpected question in that deep sensuous voice slowed her steps. His hand still held hers as she looked up at him. The blood pounded in her ears. "Not of you," she answered honestly, "but our relationship. It can't go anywhere."

His hands lifted to cradle her face. "It already has and we both know it. Maybe this will help clarify how I've felt about you from the beginning."

He lowered his dark head and gave her a slow, passionate kiss, the kind she'd been dreaming about since the moment they'd met. The hungry response she wasn't able to hold back had to leave him in no doubt why she'd returned to Patras.

A moan escaped her throat as she reeled from the intensity of long-suppressed emotions. But his kiss didn't go on and on. Instead he relinquished her mouth and lifted his head.

"I would have done this sooner, but you were too important to me to make a wrong move." She couldn't believe that's what had been in his mind. "When you said goodbye on the phone, I feared my instincts were wrong and you hadn't developed genuine feelings for me."

Zoe backed away from him, struggling for breath. "You're still not divorced."

He tipped his head, forcing her to look at him. "I thought maybe your own divorce had put you off men. Off me. I couldn't imagine any man letting you go. In time I hoped you'd open up."

She folded her arms to her waist. "I didn't ask you about your marriage for the same reason. Though a friendship had grown between us that I trusted and enjoyed, it didn't change the fact that we've both been careful not to pry beneath the surface of each other's personal lives."

"Yet you came back. Thank heaven."

CHAPTER FOUR

ZOE'S HEARTBEAT DOUBLED. She lowered her head.

"I confided in Abby. It was the first time she'd heard that I spent the month of June getting to know you while I was working. She sensed my relationship with you was important to me.

"When I told her you'd asked me not to leave because you had things to tell me, she put me on the spot about it. That's because she knew how paranoid I'd been since my divorce from Nate."

Andreas sucked in his breath. "That's the first time you've mentioned his name."

Zoe nodded. "Nate Owens."

He put a hand on her arm. "While we walk back to the car, I want to hear everything. It's growing dark."

"You're right." They'd been so deep in conversation, she hadn't noticed. To be this close to him was heavenly.

"How long since your divorce?"

"I married him at eighteen. He was twenty-five, a year younger than I am now. It lasted exactly a year and a half. Being a career pilot in the air force, he was handsome as blazes in his uniform. We met at the beach that summer while he was in Santa Monica on leave. I fell hard for him and we got married at a justice of the peace. My adoptive parents didn't approve. Neither did his family."

He stopped walking. "*Adoptive* parents?"

"Yes. Nancy and Bob Perkins, who are now divorced. He moved to his brother's place in Oregon. She still lives by the beach. I keep in touch with both of them, but they never knew anything about my own birth parents. To this day I don't have a clue about them."

"I'm sorry, Zoe." He sounded devastated for her.

"Don't be. Apparently, after I was born, I had a first set of foster parents who called me Zoe.

When I was four, I was put in the Perkinses' foster home. They eventually adopted me and gave me my last name. They also adopted two other foster children."

"Are you in touch with your siblings?"

"No. The boys were older and left at eighteen. The Perkins did their best and I owe them my life. Because of them I excelled in school and went to college. In that regard I was very blessed.

"But where my boyfriends were concerned, I thought they were too strict. When I told them that Nate wanted to marry me, Nancy said I was too young and warned me that my whirlwind romance might not work out. Bob urged me to wait and give it more time. But I didn't listen."

Andreas sat there listening.

"They were right, of course. After the wedding I fought with Nate because he wasn't ready to start a family. I caught him in half a dozen lies about other women and soon realized he wasn't ready for responsibility. His infidelity caused everything to unravel from there.

"I told him I wanted a divorce and he agreed. With no attorney involved, it didn't cost a lot to end the marriage. The experience left me wary of getting involved with another man again. You could say my stab at marriage caused me to grow up in a hurry."

"No wonder you ran from me."

By now they'd reached the car. He clicked the remote and opened the back door. Reaching for a towel he'd put on the back seat, he turned to her. "If you'll sit sideways, we'll get the sand off your feet."

Before she could say a word, he hunkered down and wiped them off. The feel of his fingers against her skin made the gesture so intimate, it sent darts of awareness through her body. Then he reached for her sandals and slipped them on for her.

"There you go."

He moved out of her way so she could stand up. While she went around to the front of the car, he used the towel on himself and put his shoes back on. When he slid behind the wheel, she reached over to squeeze his bronzed forearm.

"No one has ever treated me the way you've done. I'll never forget how you came to my rescue after that accident in the taxi. Thank you for being you." The throb in her voice seemed to reverberate in the car's elegant interior before she removed her hand.

Andreas turned on the ignition and they started back to her apartment. "Did your adoptive parents support you financially after the divorce?"

"No. They didn't have much money and I wouldn't have expected it. He worked for the post office and she ran a preschool in their modest home. They couldn't have children, so they took us all in, but I'm afraid the stress was too much for their marriage in the end."

"What amazing people."

"They were. I babysat to earn money. Later on I won some financial awards at school and received a four-year scholarship to undergraduate school at UCLA. It took care of my tuition and books.'

"Your name is Greek. It means *life*. That's one thing you're full of."

She smiled.

"You had to have been a brilliant student."

"No, just hardworking. The alimony Nate had to pay for a short period, plus my salary from working at the college bookstore, kept me afloat. I shared an old house near the campus with five other female college students so the rent was minimal. We took turns cooking."

"Who's the human dynamo of industry now?"

She laughed. "You have to understand that I became a bookworm at a very early age and I had a teacher in fourth grade who told me to study hard so I could go to college. My English teachers in junior high and high school believed I could go all the way scholastically if I didn't let anything distract me. I determined to be the top student in my field, and doors opened for me."

"That must be why you were picked to do research for the film being made."

"I guess that's true. The dean of the graduate department gave Magda Collier my name. He knew how much I'd revered Lord Byron's writings from an early age."

"He realized you were the expert, Zoe."

"In that case let's hope the film does well."

"When will it be out?"

"I don't know yet. Magda said there'd be bonuses for the girls and me. I would love to able to give some of that money to my adoptive parents. They weren't demonstrative in their affection, but the three of us knew what good people Bob and Nancy were to offer us a home during those years."

Andreas inhaled deeply. "They enabled you to become the woman you were meant to be and must feel incredibly proud of you. As for your birth parents, they would be in awe of their daughter."

She blinked hard. "If it was your intention to make me cry, you've done an excellent job of it."

* * *

Andreas drove them the rest of the way in silence. Emotion for the many struggles she'd had to overcome in this life had welled up inside him. When he found a parking spot near her flat and shut off the engine, he slid his arm along the back of the seat to face her.

In profile, her classic features had an appeal for him he never tired of studying. But now that he knew about her true parentage, he realized they had to have been exceptionally attractive people to have produced a beauty like her. They'd also endowed her with many gifts, among them unflagging perseverance and a fine mind.

"After what you've confided, I've been thinking back on my life. Under circumstances like yours, I can't imagine how I would have handled not knowing about my birth parents."

"We do what we have to. In my case I told myself not to think about it, but that wasn't possible. My siblings had a hard time, too. We had incessant conversations about it and how unfair that there were court documents that could give us answers, but they were sealed."

His dark brows lifted. "With enough money, you could probably prevail on a judge to unseal them."

"I thought about that, too, believe me. But besides the absence of that kind of money, Bob reminded me I might find out things and wish I didn't know anything."

"Do you believe that, Zoe?"

"No. I'd rather know the truth no matter what. To me, birth is a miracle. I don't care if the earth has almost eight billion people. Each person's birth is unique, *mine* most of all!"

He flashed her a tender smile. "I couldn't agree more."

"Thank you for that." She smiled back. "Even if I was a mistake, unplanned for and unwanted, or even if I was wanted but they couldn't take care of me, I would like an explanation.

"Was my dad a bookworm? Did I get my ears from my dad's mother, or my height from my mom's father? Which one had blue eyes? Did either one of them love chocolate the way I do? I guess they both had good teeth because I only have one cavity. It saved a lot of dental bills."

A chuckle escaped his throat. Her white smile was one of her extraordinary assets. Then he sobered. "Are you still tortured about it?"

"*Tortured* is too strong a word, but I admit it never left my mind growing up. It was hard to go to a girlfriend's house and see her with her real mom and dad. I never got used to that. But when I was married, Nancy gave me some advice that has stayed with me ever since."

"What was that?"

"She told me to look at it that I was given life, so make the best of it! That was Nancy. Practical and sensible. I've tried to apply it, but from time to time certain situations arise that put me in the who-am-I? mood again."

"Give me an example of what you mean. I want to understand you better."

She angled her head toward him. "From the time we met, I've wondered what it would be like to have been born a Gavras, sure of your place in life and society, secure in your family's love. Just think. Tomorrow we'll be visiting a place where your ancestors were born. Ancestors from your family line you can name and gave you identity. What greater privilege."

"I can think of one," he whispered. "Being with the woman who has brought me to a new awareness of what this life is really all about. Thank you for tonight. Your honesty has meant more to me than you know. In fact it has fortified my resolve to deal with an upcoming issue. Since it's getting late and I have to be at the office early in the morning, I'll tell you about it tomorrow."

"I'm looking forward to the trip. What time should I be ready?"

"Eight thirty. We'll eat breakfast on the plane. You have to know I don't want to leave you. The only thing that helps me is knowing you're not going anywhere except to bed. Come on. I'll walk you to the door."

He got out and helped her from the car, but didn't take her arm as they walked in order to remove himself from temptation. That kiss on the beach when he'd felt her mouth open to the pressure of his had lit a fire inside him. But it was too soon to turn it into a conflagration where they both went up in smoke.

Tonight she'd let him inside that place she'd kept hidden until now. He'd walked on sacred ground and the revelations had left him spinning. If he continued to be patient, it was possible he could convince Zoe to spend the rest of her vacation and much more with him.

Her flat door was hidden by the big tree. He waited until she'd opened it and turned on the light. It illuminated those heavenly blue eyes fringed with dark lashes. He found himself wondering which parent had endowed her with those.

When Andreas looked in the mirror, he saw a mixture of his mother and father in the reflection. His thoughts darted to his son. One day Ari would look in a mirror and not be able to find the man he thought was his father in his features or coloring. That's when Ari would want an explanation. For many reasons brought out in the conversation with Zoe, his decision to tell his son the truth about his parentage one day was more cemented than ever.

"Good night, Andreas."

"Kalinikta, kyria."

Andreas heard an awed cry from Zoe as the jet started to land. Kefalonia Island, the largest of the Ionian group, was a jewel of mountainous green with white beaches washed by brilliant clear blue water. She'd come to the island before, but by ferry. The sight from the air always took his breath.

A limo from the hotel awaited them at the airport and they were driven to the charming village of Lakithra. In a minute, the new, sprawling two-story hotel came into view, with half a dozen blue-and-white Greek flags out in front, signaling the grand opening.

"How beautiful!" Zoe exclaimed. "The yellow-and-white exterior is dazzling in the sunlight." She turned to him. "Your designer couldn't have chosen better colors for this setting. If the hotel had been here in March, I would have wanted to stay here."

"I'll pass on the compliment to the designer."

At a glance, he could tell the place was already busy. The parking lot had filled with cars and tour buses, a good sign. Several sets of visitors were going in and out. Two male hotel staff nodded to him as the chauffeur drove them under the portico to the main entrance.

They came right over to open the limo doors. "*Kalos orisate*, Kyrie Gavras."

"*Efkarista.*"

He turned to Zoe, but her attention had fastened on the entrance.

The white carved words *Gavras House, Lakithra—Lord Byron* were hung against the yellow wall on one side of the glass doors. A large, full-color picture of Lord Byron in Albanian dress hung on the other side, with white carved words beneath it: *I came here to save a country.*

"Oh, Andreas—" Without waiting for him,

Zoe climbed out past the staff and hurried over to the picture. When he joined her, she looked up at him with wet eyes. "I find it astounding that your ancestors—whose land this hotel stands on, whose blood runs through your veins—had an intimate connection with Byron."

He put a hand on her elbow, craving the warmth of the contact. "What astonishes me is that in a roundabout way covering several continents and an ocean, it brought you and me together. Shall we go inside and take a quick tour? I need to meet with the manager. After that we'll go for a walk around the village."

"This is a very exciting day for me, Andreas." Her earnestness reached his heart.

She'd dressed in a filmy white, stylish two-piece outfit suited for the eighty-nine-degree temperature. The hem of the sleeveless top hung just below her slender waist, tantalizing him. He put a hand on her back and ushered her inside. After introducing her to a handful of staff, Andreas walked her out to the inviting pool.

They had a cold drink at one of the tables,

then he introduced her in English to the manager in the office, Leon Padakis.

"Kyria Perkins is a professor of English literature at UCLA in California. She's an expert on Lord Byron."

"Ah. We're delighted that you would come to the grand opening."

"I'm thrilled to be here and love the photograph at the entrance."

His eyes twinkled. "I understand that was Kyrie Gavras's idea."

Zoe smiled at Andreas. "I knew it," she said in a low aside.

The manager gave him an inquisitive look. In Greek, he said, "She's a beautiful woman." He couldn't keep his eyes off Zoe. "I didn't know you would be coming with a guest. Will you be staying overnight?"

Andreas didn't like the man's familiarity. "We'll eat lunch in the dining room before flying back to Patras," he answered in English. "Now if you'll excuse us."

He eyed Zoe. "I know you want to revisit the Book of the Rock."

"Please."

They left the hotel and started walking. It was a favorite place of Byron's where he'd sat on some rocks and wrote his poetry. The town had erected a white stone plaque to honor him. It resembled a large book and was inscribed.

"Is everything all right, Andreas?"

"It is now." He grasped her hand and they kept on going until they reached the spot for which Lakithra was famous. She tugged on him to climb up the hill to reach the book. Then she read the Greek words aloud in English. "If I am a poet, I owe it to the air of Greece."

Zoe looked all around. "I know exactly how Byron felt. The air and the scenery here are intoxicating. What a tragedy he died young."

"We can be thankful he was prolific. After we walk to Metaxata to see his statue, we'll have a late lunch." He would just as soon not return to the hotel, but he'd come to see if its efficiency and the chef's menu were up to Gavras standards.

An hour later, as they were finishing their meal of lobster and *anginares*, she flashed him an impish smile.

"Did you know? Byron said, 'A woman should never be seen eating or drinking, unless it be lobster salad and champagne, the only truly feminine and becoming viands.' The poet had opinions on everything and hang-ups about getting fat. He'd binge, then exist on soda water and potatoes soaked in vinegar."

His black eyes smiled. "A most unusual genius."

A worried look crept into her expression. "Forgive me for going on and on, Andreas. Thank you again for bringing me here and putting up with me. While I've been relishing this unforgettable day in Byron's world, I've driven you nuts. But now I'm through and am looking forward to meeting your little boy. Does your wife know I'll be there? It might be upsetting to her."

They were finally getting around to Lia. Because Zoe was the kind of sensitive woman who had never pried into his personal life—a quality he cherished in her—she deserved to hear everything. He needed her to know all the truth.

"When we get on the plane, I'll tell you about Lia." He rang the driver to pick them up.

Her eyes reflected concern as he got to his feet and ushered her out of the dining room. With no intention of visiting the office again, Andreas walked her to the entrance. The two male staff members helped them inside the back of the limo.

During the short drive to the airport, Zoe studied him. "What's wrong, Andreas? You've been preoccupied since we first arrived at the hotel. Is it something I've done?"

"Never you." They sat by each other, making it easy for him to grasp her hand and squeeze it. "News of my separation has traveled fast. I haven't been seen in public with another woman except for you. I forgot how fast word would spread throughout the company, even to Kefalonia and a hotel manager I'd like to fire."

"What did he say to you?"

"He commented on your beauty and inferred I might want a room for the night."

"Ooh—he said that to the CEO? He really has no boundaries and doesn't know what a private person you are."

"The one thing it did do was remind me I haven't protected you from Lia. There's no doubt she's aware of you. She has eyes and ears watching me, but so far I haven't taken you to Athens."

Zoe looked stunned. "Is she the reason I haven't met your son?"

"That requires a complicated answer. I wanted you to get to know him, but at first you and I were both feeling our way carefully with each other. I feared overwhelming you."

She nodded. "How long were you married?"

"Twenty months to the day I filed for separation. I met you two days later. It's a contested divorce so I don't know when it will become final."

"I didn't realize you'd been married such a short time. I thought mine held the record for brevity but yours didn't last much longer."

"Neither marriage was meant to be," he murmured. "I'm anxious to explain everything, but we've arrived at the airport. I'll tell you the rest after we board the jet."

Andreas helped her up the steps. The elegant interior included the arrangement of four taupe-colored club seats with couches behind them. He sat across from her. Once they'd attained cruising speed and the fasten seat belt light had shut off, he leaned forward to talk to her.

"I met Lia in Athens. She was the daughter of a prominent banker I did business with in setting up an international exporting business. I fell for her.

"We didn't want a really long engagement so we were married only five months after we met. My parents had been killed in a helicopter crash the year before."

"Oh, no—" Zoe's heart ached for his loss.

"That tragedy was probably the reason I was

so eager to get married and start a family. We honeymooned in Italy, but I sensed something was wrong even then."

"Wrong? What do you mean?"

"She wasn't responsive the way she was before we got married. Sometimes I got the feeling she was avoiding me."

Zoe couldn't imagine it, not with Andreas.

"Once we realized she was pregnant, I was thrilled and thought it had to be the morning sickness affecting her. But in time I realized she wasn't going to change. By the time our son was born, we'd become completely estranged. Any joy had gone out of our marriage, but Ari brought me back to life."

"She never explained what was wrong?"

His expression grew bleak. "Never, but because of Ari I didn't want a divorce. We tolerated each other until the night he woke up screaming in pain. We rushed him to the hospital and learned he had a ruptured intestine."

"Oh, the poor little thing."

"He needed an operation and the doctor wanted our blood types."

Suddenly Zoe knew what she was going to hear. The whole time he'd been talking, she'd decided his wife had been guilt ridden over something traumatic. "Is that when you found out she had a secret?"

His gaze locked with hers. "Ari needed blood. After the operation, the doctor told me privately that he couldn't be mine."

She closed her eyes tightly. "How unbearable."

"I won't lie about that, but at least I finally understood why our marriage never worked." In the next breath he told her the rest. Lia had slept one time with another man before their wedding at a girl's bachelor party. There'd been a lot of drinking. The whole thing sickened Zoe. She couldn't imagine what it did to Andreas.

"Lia doesn't want a divorce. She has begged me to try again, but I fell out of love and the trust has completely gone out of our marriage."

"No one understands lack of trust better than I do."

"She still wants me back. At first she moved to Athens and threatened that I would never see Ari again. Of course that was absurd. The judge awarded us joint custody."

"I understand that's why you fly to Athens as often as you do."

He nodded. "He's young and I haven't wanted to take him back and forth on the jet. It's been better that I fly there. The situation has been working. I've turned the private Gavras suite at the hotel into my home away from home. But I plan to change the situation soon."

"How?"

"Lia has bought a villa in Athens and asked me for more money beyond the settlement to refurbish it. I gave it to her and pray she has already moved out of her parents' villa. The second I find out that she has, I'll take her to court for a change in visitation. We'll trade off every eight days so we both get more and equal time with Ari."

"Do you think she'll agree to it?"

"No. Lia will fight me all the way, but she'll lose because she doesn't have a job and no means of support except family money. I have the weight on my side because I earn the living.

"The judge will hear I want Ari back at the villa with me. The equal division of time every eight days means I'll be able to travel when he's not with me, and work part-time at home when he's in the house. Ari is getting older and I hope he won't mind the flights."

"If he's with you, he'll love it, Andreas. You've moved heaven and earth to make this work."

"Unfortunately it's not over yet. That's why I've told you about her. It's better to be fore-warned where Lia is concerned."

The fasten seat belt light flashed on. She buckled up. "Does the man she slept with know what happened?"

He sat back and fastened his. "It's possible, but that's a long story. I'll tell you about it on the flight to Athens in the morning when we're not rushed. Right now I must run you to the apartment because I have to get back to the office for a few hours to finish up some work."

"I understand."

In another half hour Zoe was back in the flat, wishing Andreas hadn't had to go. After kissing her cheek at the door, he'd walked swiftly away. Left to her own devices, she needed to talk to someone and pulled out her cell phone.

Eight o'clock here meant seven in Burgundy. *Abby, Abby, please be home.*

But Zoe got her voice mail and left a message to call her back. An hour later, while she was packing for the trip to Athens, she heard from her friend.

"Zoe? I've been hoping you'd call. What's happened?"

"I'm phoning to thank you for pushing me to return to Patras. I'm so glad I listened to you! I was with Andreas last evening and all day today. Tomorrow he's taking me to Athens to meet his son."

"From the sound of your voice, you're a different person."

"He…was happy I returned and we both admitted we have feelings for each other."

"Then I don't expect I'll be seeing you after all. Just promise to keep me informed when you find a moment to come down from the clouds."

"You know I will. Abby? Before we hang up, how is everything with you?"

"We've been trying for a baby. That's how it's been going."

Zoe grinned. "Lucky you."

"I'm so in love with Raoul, it's sickening. Watch out, Zoe."

"I'm afraid that warning has come too late." *Far too late*, her heart whispered. "Good luck to the two of you. I hope to hear breaking news soon! I can't help but wonder who will have a baby first. You, or Ginger."

That produced laughter from Abby before Zoe hung up and got ready for bed. She was living to be with Andreas again and feared she wouldn't be able to sleep. He'd suffered a great deal. Between the loss of his parents and Lia's betrayal, she marveled he even functioned. Then to learn

Ari wasn't his son… Only a strong, extraordinary man could deal with that.

After she climbed under the covers, oblivion eventually took over. Her watch alarm woke her up in time to shower and dress. Zoe had left out a pair of pleated cream-colored pants and a short-sleeved navy blouse. She liked its tiny print of cream and white flowers. Being around a toddler, she'd be more comfortable in this outfit.

Zoe wore earrings with a small navy blue ball hanging from a delicate gold thread. Once she'd brushed out her hair and applied pink frost lipstick, she reached for her purse and suitcase, then started out the flat door.

"Andreas—" she cried because she almost ran into him coming around the trees. His hands steadied her upper arms so she stayed upright.

"*Kalimera*, Zoe. You look incredible." He found her unsuspecting mouth and kissed her with a hunger that shook her to the depths. The passion he generated caused her to lose her grip on the suitcase and it fell to the ground. "I needed that," he said in a smoky voice against her trembling lips before picking it up for her.

Zoe took one look at him dressed in a short-sleeved coffee-colored sport shirt and white pants and almost lost her breath. No man could touch Andreas's sheer virility clothed this morning in casual elegance only he could carry off.

Andreas had come in the limo. The driver took care of her suitcase while Andreas opened the rear door. But before she could get in, he caught her to him and kissed her mouth once more.

"My marriage was over before it even began, killing the dream. I don't know about you, but the moment I found out you'd phoned my office, I started dreaming again. That in itself is a miracle. Thank heaven you're with me."

Zoe felt overwhelmed with emotion. She was a little spooked by the speed of his declarations considering how quickly she'd jumped into marriage last time. Of course it wasn't as if Andreas had asked her to marry him, but her emotions were certainly getting more complicated.

CHAPTER FIVE

ANDREAS SLID IN next to her and gripped her hand as they headed for the airport.

"You need to know what to expect when we reach Athens and are driven to the hotel. Lia always brings Ari to the private Gavras suite on the third floor. When it's time for him to go back with her, she comes to pick him up. It's her way of hoping I'll change my mind and want to get back together."

"Would you rather I went to my own room and wait until you phone me?"

"Unless you'd be too uncomfortable, I'd like you there with me. I'm positive she knows about you, but it will be a surprise to meet you. Don't let anything she says intimidate you."

"If you want to know my greatest fear, it's that I'll say or do something that will upset your son. Since I only know a few words in Greek, you'll have to translate."

"That'll be a pleasure. When you hand him the gift bag, he'll be too excited with the present to notice anything else. You were inspired."

"When I bought it, I had no idea I would ever meet him. He sounds like a typical child."

"Besides toys, Ari loves games, especially hide-and-seek."

Before long they reached the airport and he helped her up the steps of the jet. Andreas asked the steward to serve them breakfast once they were in the air. The flight lasted only forty-five minutes and there were things he needed to talk to her about before they landed.

After the trays had been removed, he walked her to one of the couches and pulled her down next to him. "I have a fear greater than yours, Zoe. I'm taking you into what could be a difficult situation, but I despise secrets."

"You'll get no argument from me there. I imagine this has to do with Ari's birth father."

"You told me I was intuitive, but I think it's

the other way around. Lia wouldn't talk about it, so through the PI I hired, I learned he comes from a well-known French shipping family from Marseilles, but I don't know his name.

"Depending on what kind of a man he is and his circumstances, he might want to share custody of Ari. Or there's the possibility he might fight for full custody of him. Then again, he might not be interested at all. That's what Lia believes—or would like to believe, anyway."

Zoe lowered her head. "I can't imagine a father not wanting to claim his own flesh and blood, but there must be thousands of cases where we know it happens."

Andreas nodded. "The point is, Lia doesn't want him to know anything. She's terrified of scandal and how it will affect her parents, who are well-known in Athens society. She has begged me to take her back."

"I don't doubt it for a second, Andreas. I'm sure she does regret what she did."

"Obviously. But what she needs to realize is that he has a right to know he has a son."

"He does!" Zoe blurted with all the emotion in her.

"When I warned Lia I'd discovered Ari's father's identity and would let the man know the truth if she didn't, she threatened again to sue for full custody."

Zoe turned to him. He could feel her body trembling. "She couldn't take him away from you."

"True. The law wouldn't allow it, but she turned the situation ugly when she left for Athens. She knew my headquarters were in Patras."

A sigh escaped Zoe's lips. "If she thought to defeat you by making it harder for you to be with Ari, then she didn't know you at all." Those blue eyes darkened with pain for him. "Did this Guion know she was engaged to you?"

"Lia said she took her ring off at the party, but I can't imagine him not knowing."

"I can't either, not when she was going to be married to someone as renowned as you. Everyone in her circle of friends who attended the party had to know she was playing with fire. What kind of a man would do that?" Zoe sounded angry.

"I don't know what he's like," Andreas muttered. "He had to have been acquainted with Lia's best friend, Eliana, who held the yacht party. I asked Lia if she thought Eliana knew Ari wasn't mine. She said she probably did, but Eliana would never say anything. You and I both know she could tell him at any moment."

"But if that were true, don't you think you would have heard from him by now?"

"I don't know, but I refuse to live my life worrying that one day down the road, I'm going to get a phone call from his attorney because Lia kept the truth from him. She doesn't realize that if she stays silent and he finds out anyway, it could turn on her."

Zoe moaned. "If handled wrong, it would be traumatic for all three of you, not to mention the turmoil on the birth father's side."

"That's why he needs to know the truth right away."

"I couldn't agree more, Andreas. The news

might bring him joy, even if it's tearing you apart."

He put his arm around her shoulders and pulled her closer. "I knew you'd say that. You've had your whole life to wade through the depths of not knowing your parentage. Don't worry about me. I've had time since the day of the operation to consider the fact that I might have to share Ari's love."

"Do your grandparents know?"

"Yes. They're devastated, but they understand it has to be done. Naturally when Ari is old enough to comprehend, he'll be told. Maybe by me or Lia, or by the father himself. After hearing your heart-wrenching story, I want Ari to know everything he can about the blood flowing through his veins when he's ready. He has grandparents, uncles and aunts, cousins, maybe half brothers or sisters he isn't aware of."

Zoe hugged him, but he had to let her go. The fasten seat belt sign had gone on. Andreas kissed the side of her face before helping her buckle up. "We've started our descent."

"I didn't even notice the sign."

"That's because you were too busy comforting me." Zoe's compassion was a revelation to him.

In a few minutes they landed and the steward carried their luggage to the limo waiting for them. The three-story Gavras House—Athens was built along nineteenth-century neoclassic lines—was hardly the place for a growing toddler, but it served Andreas's purpose for the time being. He'd arranged for Zoe's room on the second floor near the elevator for easy access.

They went to hers first.

"Look at those fresh flowers!" she exclaimed in delight when they walked in the sitting room off the bedroom. "Daffodils and daisies." Zoe turned to him. "You had these sent to me?"

The smile on her face made the effort worth it. He lowered her suitcase. "In Greece the two together express hope and new beginnings. Today represents both since you're about to meet my son."

For a moment her eyes searched his. "How

beautiful! I love them. Give me a moment to freshen up. I'll be right back."

True to her word, she was gone only a couple of minutes. After walking over to inspect the flowers one more time, she went with him to his suite on the floor above.

When they walked in the front room, she halted. "You've transformed this into a child's paradise!"

"Hardly that. All I've done is replicate what he was used to at the villa. It'll go back with us when visitation is changed." He carried his suitcase over to the couch. After he pulled out the gift bag, he put it on the coffee table. "Excuse me for a minute."

Andreas took his suitcase in the bedroom. When he returned, he noticed she'd been drawn to the drum with the large colored circles. She'd knelt and was pressing one sound after another. Zoe smiled up at him. "I've never seen such a cute toy. Does he love it?"

"Not as much as that wooden wagon with the blocks. He has a routine of taking a few out, leaving them and moving on before he removes some more. When they're all on the floor, he methodically starts picking them up."

"Maybe he'll run his own delivery service one day. A chip off the old block. Gavras International Express Mail," she teased.

"That's a thought." While they both laughed, he heard the familiar knock. "They're here," he murmured. Zoe got to her feet, still holding the drum. "Ready?"

She nodded.

Zoe's heart thudded as he opened the door. She watched his dark-headed boy reach for Andreas, who swept him up in his arms. He spoke Greek to him in endearing terms and heard Ari say *baba* several times as they hugged.

Lia, a tall, stunning brunette, walked past them dressed in a becoming pink sundress with spaghetti straps. She'd seen Zoe and made her way toward her. Thank heaven Andreas had prepared her for what Lia might do.

He closed the gap, still carrying Ari. "Lia?

This is Zoe Perkins, a friend of mine from the US. She's a professor of English literature at UCLA."

"So I've heard."

Andreas had been right. His wife had already been informed.

"Zoe? May I introduce Ari's mother and our son."

"It's nice to meet you, Kyria Gavras." His wife was still a Gavras.

"How do you do, Kyria Perkins?" Lia spoke English well.

"You have an adorable boy."

"Thank you."

Zoe smiled at their son. "*Yassou*, Ari." She'd been practicing a few words, "hello" being one of them.

Ari stared at the drum she was holding and squirmed to get down. Andreas lowered him to the floor. Zoe immediately handed it to him and he sat to play with it. She had an idea he hadn't liked her holding it. Deciding now was as good a time as any, she reached for the gift bag on the coffee table and put it on the floor in front of him.

He was so cute when he looked up at her in surprise. Zoe hunkered down and pulled out the gift Andreas had rewrapped. "This is for you." She started to undo it, then left it to him to finish, all the while aware his mother was watching.

Ari made fast work of it and out came the three ModMobiles on wheels. With the same methodical precision Andreas had told her about, he lined them up and pushed them around on his hands and knees. Zoe intercepted a warm glance from Andreas.

"How long will you be in Greece?" This from Lia. The tension was growing.

Zoe stood up, needing an answer to that herself. "I'm not sure."

To her relief Andreas said something to Lia in Greek and started walking her to the door. For the moment Ari didn't seem to notice. He was too concentrated on his new toys.

When Andreas stepped out in the hall, Zoe

got down on her knees again and turned one of the toys around. Next, she pushed it against the second one. Ari lifted his head and stared at her before he pushed the third one into hers. She reached for the first one and war broke out. Every time she hit one of his, he laughed a little and hit back.

Pretty soon Andreas joined them and turned it into a battle until Ari laughed so hard he got the hiccups. Clearly he adored his daddy.

"It's time for his lunch. Let's go down to the restaurant. Then we'll come back and play until he's ready for his nap. I set up a crib in the second bedroom with his favorite stuffed bear and rabbit."

"I can tell it won't be long before he climbs out of it."

Andreas grinned. "I'm expecting to hear a thump any day now. When he's back home with me, he'll have a regular bed."

Lunch turned out to be a hilarious experience. Andreas made a game out of everything. The love he showered on his son was something to behold. After they returned to the living room, Zoe straightened things while he put his son down.

"Sorry it took so long."

She looked up at him from the couch. He stood there with his legs slightly apart, her idea of the ultimate male. "It's not surprising. If I'd had that much stimulation from a doting father, I would never have wanted to go to bed either. He's precious, Andreas."

"You were wonderful with him."

"Thank goodness he didn't act frightened around me."

"Anything but."

"Was Lia upset?"

"Yes. After seeing you, she informed me she needs more money before she can move. I told her there was no more and I'd see her the day after tomorrow at the same time when she comes for Ari.

"While he's asleep I'm going to phone Yorgos. He'll fax my change of visitation petition to her attorney today and demand the soonest court date possible for the ruling."

She feared the agony Andreas suffered would continue for a long time yet. "What if she won't agree to it?"

"For all the obvious reasons, the judge will rule in my favor and she'll have to comply. Will you excuse me while I disappear in my bedroom for a few minutes?"

"Of course. I have a phone call of my own to make."

"Abby or Ginger?"

She chuckled. "Neither one. The new Signora della Scala is still on her honeymoon. When she returns, we three girls will have a long conversation. In the meantime it occurred to me I haven't checked in with Harriet at the office in months."

"Harriet?"

"The secretary at UCLA. She'll know if the August date has been set for the faculty party the dean gives to start off the fall semester. If there's any interesting news, Harriet will pass it on. The department couldn't function without her."

He was quiet for a moment before he said, "After being away from teaching this long, are you anxious to get back to it?"

What would Andreas say if she told him she never wanted to leave him? "To be honest, I've been having such a wonderful time here with you, I haven't really thought about it."

"That's good because I have more things planned for us with Ari, *and* when we're alone," he added in a low tone. Her heart turned over. Those words would have filled her with pure joy but for the presence of Lia. His wife wasn't through trying to convince Andreas to make their marriage work. Why else was she doing everything possible to hang on to him?

"I can't wait to see Athens with the two of you. It'll be much different from when I was living in a apartment here doing research."

"That I can promise." His black eyes gleamed. "Ari won't sleep more than an hour. One of these days he'll outgrow his naps, too."

"I did a lot of babysitting and know it happens faster than you think."

"Which is why I want him for longer periods."

"I totally understand that."

"When he wakes up, we'll go to the zoo and ride the train. With you along, it'll make a whole new, exciting adventure for him." He paused. "Miss me while I'm in the other room?"

Andreas...

The next two days turned out to be the happiest Zoe had ever known. Andreas was so relaxed while they played with Ari, he seemed to have thrown off his concerns and looked younger. Zoe never forgot for a second she wasn't Ari's mother, but she treasured these moments he allowed her to share with them.

After Ari went down at night, they spent both evenings in his suite watching home movies taken at his breathtaking villa. They showed Ari at every stage of development. Zoe saw his grandparents and other relatives. Lia appeared in them, too.

They were the picture of the perfect family,

but Andreas announced there were no more movies once they'd taken Ari home from the hospital. Learning the truth had made a total shambles of his world. As soon as Ari had recovered from the operation, he'd filed for a divorce and Lia had moved to Athens. How to be with his son was all that had consumed him.

Both nights when Zoe left his suite for her own room, he walked her to the door and kissed her hungrily. But he didn't pull her back into his arms and keep her there. This trip to Athens had been primarily for her to meet Ari.

Zoe also suspected he was anxious for Lia to see that Ari would always be an integral part of his life while he moved on with other women. Though Zoe had been the first since Andreas's divorce, she still had no idea what the future held for either of them.

If there was any trauma, it happened when Lia appeared at the hotel door to pick up Ari. Zoe hung back while Andreas walked him to his mother. She quickly reached for him and said something in Greek, giving him a kiss.

Ari kissed her back, then wiggled to get down. Lia held him tighter and he started crying out *baba*. Then he saw Zoe and she heard him call out her name for the first time.

It thrilled her because Andreas had been teaching Ari to say it. But for his son to do it in front of Lia probably killed her. She loved her little boy. That much was clear before she hurried away with him. Even though Andreas shut the door, they could both hear him having hysterics in the hallway.

Andreas turned to her. His pained expression tore at her heart. "Let's go down to your room for your suitcase. The limo is waiting out in front." He couldn't leave Athens fast enough and she didn't blame him. More than ever Zoe understood why he wanted his son for longer periods in his own villa in Patras.

She found a plastic bag and brought the flowers he'd given her with them.

On the way to the airport she brought up something maybe she would regret, but she couldn't bear to see him this stressed. This time he sat across from her, totally preoccupied.

"Would it be impossible for you to move your headquarters here and buy a home until he's a little older? You could see him two or three times a week and every other weekend with no flying involved."

She heard him groan. "That was Lia's grand design when she moved here, but Athens isn't my home. I identify with my western roots and want that for Ari. To uproot the company and my other business would be pure folly, and—" He stopped short. "Forgive me, Zoe. You have the misfortune of seeing me at my wretched worst."

"There's nothing to forgive. When Ari had to leave you a little while ago, he wasn't in the greatest mood either. Talk about two peas in a pod."

He shook his head. "Have you forgotten we're—"

"Don't say it!" she broke in on him. "You *are* father and son. I was there. That vital, emotional bond forged before he was born is DNA deep. He idolizes you. I saw moments when he tried to imitate you."

"In what way?"

She had his attention at last. "How you throw a ball, and some of the sounds you make while you're teasing each other. If you're afraid he doesn't look like you, that's the least of your worries. A lot of people don't resemble their parents. But take it from me. I know a good-looking man when I see one, and he's already a heartthrob."

Just like you.

Andreas sat back, staring at her through narrowed lids. "You always manage to say the right thing. Thank heaven for you. If you're not sick of me yet, would you consider taking a little trip with me after we get back to Patras?"

It was a good thing he wasn't sitting next to her. His question caused a sudden surge of adrenaline igniting her body he would surely have felt. "Is it for your work?"

"Sometimes I do things for pleasure. I'd like

to take you out on my boat overnight. I'll show you the delights of the gulf and beyond. It's home to the striped and common dolphins, a treat you'll enjoy. We'll do some swimming and snorkeling. Anything we want. How does that sound?"

Too good to be true. "Can you take that time away from the office?"

A frown marred his striking features. "Is that your way of saying you'd rather not come with me?"

"Andreas—" She sat forward, gripping the sides of the chair. "I'm trying to be considerate when you have so many calls on your time."

"Then I'll ask you again and would like a simple answer."

He really was in a mood. "Yes. I'd love to go."

"That's all I needed to hear. We'll eat lunch on the plane. When we get back to Patras, I have to go into the office, but only for a few hours."

"I thought so."

"I promise I won't be long. After I come by

for you, we'll pick up some groceries and drive to the port. I'm a pretty good cook."

"That sounds exciting. But if we're going to be on the water, then we'll share the meal making. Can we fish?"

"I know spots to find red snapper and cod with my spinning rod."

"Fabulous. We'll eat what we catch. I wish we were there already."

"I'm way ahead of you."

CHAPTER SIX

"You call this a boat?" A light sea breeze tousled Zoe's dark blond hair as her gaze darted everywhere.

Andreas had just given her a tour. "That's what it is."

"You're a master of understatement. This is a sleek, oceangoing, state-of-the-art yacht."

"It only has two bedrooms."

She rolled her eyes, more brilliant a blue than the gulf itself. "Plus two bathrooms, a closet, a kitchen with a washer and dryer, and a sitting room with built-in office equipment."

"Yet it's small enough I can man it myself. I don't want a crew."

"I don't blame you. When you want to escape, you have a self-contained world that's all yours.

I noticed the name on the side and wish I could read Greek. Will you translate it for me?"

"*Amphitrite*, goddess of the sea and Poseidon's wife."

"I should have known it would be something deliciously Greek."

Not as delicious as she was. Andreas handed her a life jacket from one of the cubbies on the top deck near the banquette. She put it on over her stunning figure clad in jeans and a white pullover.

"Does Ari love it already?"

"I haven't brought him out on it."

"Why not?"

"Lia had a brother who never learned how to swim and drowned years ago. After Ari was born, she made me promise we wouldn't take him on the *Amphitrite* until he could swim with-out a life preserver."

"I can understand that. How sad for her and her family."

"I've moved him around in the villa pool. When visitation is changed and he's home with me for whole weeks at a time, I'll start to have fun in the water with him."

"He'll adore it."

"We'll see how soon he learns to swim. For this trip I'm looking forward to swimming with *you*. Come and sit near me." He'd undone the ropes and was ready to cast off.

She did his bidding. "You don't know how excited I am. It's wonderful to be finished with the research project and not worry about anything for a while."

"I need time off, too."

"Since knowing you, I've seen how hard you work. You have the energy of a dozen men."

Andreas flashed her a smile. He'd wanted to be with her like this after he'd first met her, but instinct had told him to go slow. When she'd left him so suddenly for Venice, he'd felt too gutted to believe it. But she'd come back! There was no way he was going to let her go again.

"I'd like to reach a certain cove where we can lay anchor and catch some cod for our dinner. They'll be biting this time of evening."

Andreas turned the key and eased them out beyond the buoy. The engine ran so quietly, he felt and heard her suck in her breath with pleasure when he opened up the throttle. They flew across the water.

"That dial says the temperature is a fabulous eighty-six degrees! With the gulf so calm, this would be the best possible place to water-ski." Her enthusiasm for everything enamored him. She loved life and he loved being with her.

Strange how he'd thought his love was strong for Lia before their marriage. But he hadn't met Zoe then. The speed of his feelings for her had taken him by complete surprise. Her strength of character, her compassion and kindness made her a woman above others. In every atom of his body he knew he wanted to go through life with her.

"I'll take you tomorrow with dolphins swimming all around you."

A full smile broke out on her beautiful face. "Now I know I'm dreaming. Please don't ever let me wake up."

Not a chance. His exhilaration at being with her was over the top. "I'm in it with you, remember?"

He drove the boat up the coast while she soaked in the scenery. When they came to his favorite spot in a quiet cove, he shut off the motor. Next to an outcropping of rocks was a sandy patch of beach. Andreas was pleased no one else was here and they could be alone.

Zoe let out a squeal of delight and walked over to the side of the boat. After he lowered the anchor, he moved behind her and kissed the back of her neck. That brought her around into his arms where he wanted her. "I can't wait for this any longer."

"Andreas—"

He smothered her cry, needing to taste her the way he needed air to breathe. She melted against him, going where he led, giving him kiss for kiss. They both lost track of time and place, trying to satisfy their needs.

When he realized they needed to breathe, he relinquished her luscious mouth. "I could engulf you, Zoe. This life jacket is the only thing saving me from losing complete control."

With her hands on his chest, she gazed at him with a come-hither smile she couldn't have been aware of. "But *you're* not wearing one." She slid her hands around his neck and began kissing every part of his face. The touch of her roving lips against his skin spiked his desire. If he'd wanted proof that her hunger matched his, he didn't need to wait any longer.

A fire had been lit a long time ago. It had been burning steadily beneath the surface, finding an opening here and there to allow bursts of flame to escape and grow. "Will it frighten you if I tell you how much I want you?"

His question caused her to stop kissing him. She looked into his eyes. Her hands slid back to his chest. "I confess that the instant we met, I was strongly attracted to you, too. That has never changed. But it frightens me that the time will come when your ardor for me cools."

Her honesty caused his body to tauten. He

clutched her tighter. "Do you know something I don't?"

"I've gone into this with my eyes wide open, Andreas. Unless you weren't telling me the truth, I'm the first woman you've been with since the moment you told your wife you were divorcing her."

"Are you saying you doubt me?"

"No. Otherwise I wouldn't be here now. But it's common knowledge that divorced people need time to find out who they are. I've been single a long time. At this point I know who I am. Unlike you, I've had opportunities to meet other men. So far none have been important to me.

"However, you're still reeling from your separation that only happened recently. You haven't had enough time to get your feet on the ground."

That was where she was wrong. "Try nearly twenty-two months. Perhaps I haven't made it clear that the sexual side of our marriage was never satisfactory. After Lia told me she was pregnant, there was no intimacy between us, not ever again. And now we know why. I've had a lot more time to think about the future during my soulless, defunct marriage than you can imagine."

Zoe averted her eyes. "I didn't realize that, but it doesn't change the fact that other women will come into your life while you're making a home for you and Ari."

"I've been surrounded by beautiful females for years, wherever I'm working."

"I don't doubt it, but you know what I meant."

"Whatever you were insinuating, you'd be wrong. Don't confuse me with your ex-husband."

She closed her eyes tightly for a moment. "I promise I'm not, Andreas."

He believed her. "Tell me something. Where do you think *you're* going to be while I'm getting my feet firmly on the ground?"

A tiny nerve throbbed at the base of her creamy throat. "I have a job to return to in California."

That's what you think.

Being a foster child had deprived her of a feeling of permanence before she'd been adopted. Add to that, a marriage at a young age with a pilot who was incapable of putting down roots had made her skittish.

Andreas didn't question why she'd kept herself from getting too close to any man again. Many opportunities had to have been there. The more he thought about it, the more he realized it was a miracle she'd come back to Patras after she'd fled to her friends in Venice. He didn't care what excuse she'd used for her return. Deep in his soul he knew she hadn't been able to walk away from him.

"What's your timeline?"

"I don't have one, not yet. Right now I'm here with you and loving every minute of it."

The frank admission, not easily given, sent a new burst of longing to reveal things she still didn't know, but he had to take it step by step. "I'm glad to hear it. We still have a lot to talk about, but we'll do it later because I'm getting hungry for dinner."

Her eyes sparkled. "Me, too."

"What do you say I put the right lure on the line of your pole and we'll see what's out there?"

He led her to the back near the transom where he kept his spinning rods. Andreas opened his large tackle box.

"Good heavens—you have so many different lures, you must fish a lot."

"I've done my share over the years with friends and family. While you inspect them, I'll go below and bring up a small cooler filled with ice."

He hurried down the gangway and was back in a minute. "Have you found one you like?"

"This black one with the pink spots speaks to me."

"I'm afraid that little beauty won't catch cod, maybe a sea bass. But they don't hang out here."

"So which of these has the magic?"

"We'll try this one." He reached for the orange eel jig and fastened it to the line. "If I put on a bullet weight, it'll sink to the right depth.

After you cast and start to reel in, the eel will wiggle and flash, driving the cod crazy."

She let out a happy laugh. "I can't wait to watch it work. Will you cast first? I want to see you do it."

This was beyond fun. Andreas set it all up and gave her a demonstration, but the lure came in empty. "I'll try it again." In the end he had to cast four times before he felt that tug. "Got one!"

Zoe actually jumped with excitement while he slowly reeled it in. Out came a nine-inch cod. "That's a perfect size!"

He hit it on the head. Once he removed the lure, he put his catch in the cooler. Then he re-attached the lure and handed her the rod. "I've caught my dinner. Now it's your turn. That is if you want to eat," he baited her.

"Oh, brother." She squinted her eyes at him. "You just watch." She imitated his technique as best she could and ended up casting five times without success. "What am I doing wrong?"

"Not a thing. I can tell you've fished before."

"Nate took me out on a boat with some of his friends, but it was a long time ago."

"Did you have success?"

"Not that I can remember."

Andreas smiled. "Just keep trying. Maybe a different spot."

"Good idea." She turned and cast to the left side of the boat. It wasn't long before she cried out, "I've got a fish!"

"Keep reeling it in," he said, happy for her.

Pretty soon she lifted it from the water. "It's smaller than yours, but I'll keep it."

"Only by an inch. We have the right amount for our meal." He took care of the cod, but had to reach for his fishing knife to remove the hook of the lure.

"My poor little fish didn't stand a chance."

Andreas chuckled and put it in the cooler. She straightened his tackle box and put it away along with the pole.

"Let's go below. I'll gut the fish and put them on the grill."

"While you do that I'll start the potatoes and onions."

"When we're ready to eat, we'll watch the moon fall into the sea. There's no sight like it."

His black eyes wandered over her. They gleamed with such intensity, she hoped her legs wouldn't give out on her. With Andreas, no experience would ever be the same again. Being with him had colored her world for all time.

I'm fatally in love. The worst kind. When I'm back in California it will haunt me forever. But, fool that I am, until I leave Greece I intend to enjoy this time with you to the fullest.

Zoe hurried down the gangway to freshen up. When she entered the galley where she'd put the flowers he'd given her, she noticed he'd already cleaned the fish and was preparing the grill.

"You work fast. Why doesn't that surprise me?"

He darted her an enticing smile. "I put out the skillet. The potatoes and onions are next to the cutting board. What else do you need?"

"Olive oil and a knife to begin with."

Andreas found both items for her and she got busy. They worked in harmony. Once the vegetables had started to fry, she reached in the fridge for butter. "I'm going to need salt."

He handed her a small jar from the shelf. Zoe looked at the label, which was printed in Greek, of course. When she took off the lid, she darted him a glance. "What kind of salt is this?"

"Sea salt, the purest of all salts."

"I've never cooked with it before." She sprinkled a little over the vegetables.

"It's healthier than iodized salt and contains essential trace minerals our bodies need to stay healthy."

Zoe stared at him. "How do you know so much about it?"

One of his black brows lifted devilishly. "If you *could* read Greek, you'd see that the manufacturer is A. Gavras, Messolonghi, Greece."

"You're in the sea salt business?"

He nodded. "At an early age my father warned me not to put my all my proverbial eggs in one basket or depend on the family hotel business to be there forever."

"Your father was a wise sage."

"I idolized him, so I invested all my earnings growing up and didn't touch them."

She smiled at him. "If every child were so intelligent." The potatoes and onions were almost done.

"Don't forget I didn't have siblings. He was my world. In college I had a business professor who challenged the class to look for opportunities that weren't necessarily high-tech or bitcoin ventures."

"That's unconventional thinking."

"He sounded like my father." By now Andreas had started grilling the fish. "I'd been working at our hotel in Messolonghi at the time and heard about a failing pharmaceutical plant sitting on property near the port. The owner had fallen into desperate financial trouble.

"On a whim I got in touch with the law firm handling the matter and was given a walk-through."

"Not a whim," Zoe broke in. "Sheer inspiration from a fine mind who'd inherited your father's business acumen. I'm so impressed you can't imagine."

"Don't be. It could easily have failed."

"But it didn't, or I wouldn't be holding this jar in my hand. Tell me what happened."

"I realized that new ownership could use the facilities for something different, yet substantial. I got in touch with one of the scientists who'd worked there. He told me he would have given anything to buy the whole place and turn it into a sea salt business. But he didn't have the money."

Zoe moved the skillet off the burner. "I want to hear the details."

"We had a lot of conversations. The more we talked, the more I was convinced it could work. There was all the seawater in the world. It was free. But to convert it meant boiling it down. That took fuel, and it costs a lot of money."

"And Andreas Gavras, being the obedient son who'd saved his money, could provide it and turn it into a business that wasn't high-tech or related to your family's business. You're so brilliant it's scary."

Rich laughter burst from Andreas. "After talking it over with my father, I bought the property and hired the scientist to help me find the right people to get it started."

"I can't comprehend putting a business like that together."

"It was an enormous undertaking. I had to fund employees with insurance and benefits. Besides making the product, I had to decide where to sell it. Advertising costs had to be entered into the budget in order to get it off the ground. That meant hiring a marketing manager to laud the features of sea salt. Did you know it provides electrolytes that maintain water balance and assist in nerve and muscle function?"

She laughed. "You know very well I know nothing about it."

"Neither did I, which was why I had to surround myself with experts. After deciding I would sell to clients in Europe, I had to make arrangements to ship our product using trucks and trains. In order to reach the countries around the Mediterranean, I had to negotiate with different shipping lines that would come to the port of Messolonghi."

"This isn't lip service when I tell you it's a marvel what you've done."

He leaned over and kissed the side of her brow. "If I've loaded you with too much information, there's a reason. Ten years ago I did business with the CEO of Norville Shipping out of Marseilles, France. It's been going strong ever since."

"Wait a minute, a shipping line in Marseilles?" She gasped the name once she'd connected the dots. "Do you mean that Ari's dad is…?"

He nodded when he saw she'd figured it out. "How's that for a twist of irony? Out of all the men Lia could have picked…"

"But you never met him."

"No. The CEO I did business with was probably his grandfather. They have the kind of money that would enable him to come after

Lia if he finds out she had his baby and didn't tell him.

"I'm waiting to hear how soon the judge will rule on my change of visitation petition. If Lia does anything to hold it up, then I'm not going to wait any longer to meet with Norville."

Her stomach clenched in worry for him.

"Zoe? I'd like your input on how best to approach him."

"Oh, Andreas—I don't know."

"I can't think of anyone whose opinion I would value more. And I'd like you to go to France with me."

While she stood there speechless, he found a tray, cutlery and two plates. It dawned on her the food was ready. Together they served up the fish and potatoes. She put on a lemon garnish and fresh plums and added some Halloumi cheese rolls.

He gave her a sideward glance. "I'll carry this up if you'll bring the wine and glasses."

Zoe fairly trembled as she gathered those last items and followed him to the deck. They sat on a banquette with the tray between them. She found a spot for the glasses and Andreas poured them Moschofilero white wine he'd said came from the finest vineyards in the southern Peloponnese region of Greece.

He raised his glass to her. "You'll taste peppermint, rose and citrus, elements of my homeland. It will enhance the flavor of our little two-year-old cod fish, born and raised here in Grecian waters."

"Two-year-olds?"

"Their great-grandparents are around here somewhere and probably six feet long by now."

She chuckled softly and lifted her glass. "To hope and new beginnings."

He touched her glass with his own. "Thank you for coming with me." His deep voice resonated inside her body.

"It's a privilege for me, Andreas."

After they drank some of the delicious wine, they began eating. It tasted so good she couldn't stop until there was nothing left. He'd eaten all of his, too.

She lifted her eyes to him. "You probably won't believe me, but that's the best meal I ever had in my life."

"You just read my mind. Now, take a look at the horizon."

She turned to the west just as the half-moon started sliding into the water. The surreal night was so mystical, she felt the hairs rise on the back of her neck.

"What is it about beauty that makes you hurt?"

"That's what happens to me when I look at you."

"Too much wine again," she quipped, "but I'm a woman who likes to hear it anyway."

"You have a hard time accepting a compliment." His gaze studied her profile, making her restless. "What's your answer, Zoe?"

She felt her heart palpitate. "To which question?"

"Both. How to approach Norville and if you'll come to France with me? I've made inquiries through a private detective I've used and trusted here in Patras, Gus Paulos. He told me Guion lives in Nice. Apparently he worked in the shipping business, then real estate. Now he dabbles in other things."

"Is he married?"

"Twice, and separated from his second wife."

Zoe sucked in her breath. "So he's had a divorce."

"Yes."

"Does he have children?"

"One from each marriage, so Gus tells me. Tomorrow I'll find out if my attorney has good news for me and Lia has agreed to the terms. If not, then I'm going to take matters into my own hands. I want you with me."

After Andreas talked to the other man, he would learn he had another child.

"I can hear what you're thinking," he murmured. "This couldn't be a more difficult time for Norville to get news like this."

"No. But I don't suppose there's ever a right time."

Andreas looked out over the water. "Knowing

what I've told you, do you still feel he should be told?"

"I wish you hadn't asked me that. I'm seeing this from Ari's side. If he learns through you about his birth father, he'll love you for being honest no matter how shocking the news is to him. But if he finds out first that you're not the one who gave him life, I imagine he'll feel betrayed by both you and his mother."

"In other words, whatever Norville's circumstances, you're still of the opinion I should tell him."

"Yes."

"I feel exactly the same way. Now I'm trying to decide how I'd like to be contacted about this if I were Norville. Any thoughts you have on the matter will be greatly appreciated."

"Let me think about it tonight, Andreas."

"Will you fly to Nice with me?"

She got up from the banquette and reached for the glasses and wine bottle that was still two-thirds full. "I'll tell you my answer in the morning."

Zoe went down to the galley and started to clean up. In a minute he joined her and put their plates in the dishwasher. When she'd finished, she turned to him. "If you don't mind, I'm going to bed. I don't have to tell you it's been a glorious day."

Lines darkened his features. "It was until I mentioned Norville."

Her head came up. "How could you not? Your life can't move on until this issue is resolved. To my mind the sooner the better. Ari is the most important person in this whole equation. Good night."

Zoe walked past Andreas to reach her cabin. He didn't try to stop her. Long after she got ready for bed, she lay there in a quandary thinking about her own life. Her birth parents had disregarded her. As for her first set of foster parents, the only thing Nancy had told her about them was that they had run into financial difficulties and the state had needed to step in to find Zoe a new home.

Though her situation and Ari's were entirely different, she knew he would face some struggles growing up and it was vital that Andreas focus on him right now rather than Zoe.

Andreas had been so intent on being with her since they met, she wondered if it was his way of distracting himself from the stressful things going on in his life right now. Given time, he might not even want or need Zoe in his life the same way.

She'd thrown caution to the wind and had come back to Patras desperate to see Andreas once more. All it had accomplished was to prove how deeply in love she was with him. Meeting his son had added another layer to cement her feelings for him.

But in asking her to fly to France with him, he'd put her on a precipice. There was no safety net below. No guarantees where their relationship was headed.

To put her heart at risk again was asking too

much when so much more stood in the way of her happiness with Andreas. Not knowing what was in store, Zoe was frightened to get any more involved with him. She couldn't do it and slept poorly the rest of the night.

CHAPTER SEVEN

ANDREAS SPENT AN agonizing night on deck. He doubted that he'd slept at all. Before Zoe left the galley, he should have stopped her and told her everything going on inside him. Instead, he'd asked her to go to Nice with him to face an uncertain outcome involving his son.

He thought back to the moment when Zoe had returned from Italy. When he'd pressed her, she'd admitted to having developed deeper feelings for him and had been afraid of them. But she'd had to come back to tell him.

Her honesty had overjoyed him because of his love for her. But he hadn't said or done enough to reassure her about the future he wanted with her. With his life so unsettled, how could she be confident of anything?

Once the sun rose over the horizon, he went

below to shower and shave. After putting on khaki shorts and a white T-shirt, he went in the galley to fix breakfast for them. They would eat at the table.

An hour later she appeared at the entrance dressed in pink shorts and a white T-shirt. Their tops were the same, but her feminine shape almost caused him to drop his coffee mug. Could there be a more beautiful woman?

"Mmm. Something smells mouthwatering."

"I've made you my recipe for Greek coffee to start our day. The kind with the grounds on the bottom and foam on top. Sit down and I'll serve you."

"Thank you. After that dinner last night, I can't believe I'm hungry again."

"I'm glad. I've put out pastries and yogurt to go with the eggs." He brought everything to the table he'd already set.

She flashed him a smile before sitting on one of the chairs. He straddled one opposite her and they both began to eat.

Halfway through their meal she said, "My compliments to the chef. This is delicious."

"Thank you."

"I meant it. To what do I owe this honor? Is there anything you can't do?"

He'd finished the last of his pastry. "Let me ask you a question first. A while back you said you'd been single a long time and at this point knew who you were."

A confused expression broke out on her face. He'd caught her off guard. "I remember."

"Do you know yourself well enough to imagine spending the rest of your life with me?"

If he wasn't mistaken, she lost some color.

"Zoe—it should be patently clear by now that I'm in love with you."

She shook her head. "You think you are. It's always that way in the beginning of a relationship, especially if you've just come out of an unhappy marriage."

He could see he had a fight on his hands. "Forget that I haven't had three years to find out who I really am. That's not me. My big mistake was letting you leave for Venice without telling you how I felt from the start. But with certain matters in my life not yet resolved, I worried the truth would scare you off. When you came back, I knew someone upstairs was on my side."

She couldn't meet his eyes. "I should have gone to France with Abby."

"Maybe you didn't hear me the first time. I want to marry you, Zoe Perkins. Because of circumstances, it won't be today or tomorrow, but soon. Last night I made another mistake by asking you to fly to Nice with me without you knowing my deepest feelings."

This time when she looked at him, her blue eyes were shimmering with unshed tears. There was a frightened woman inside her. "You don't know what you're saying."

"The hell I don't! The other day when you mentioned calling the secretary at the university to find out about the faculty party, it was like my worst nightmare. If you think I'm going to let you get away from me again, then you don't know me. When you left the first time, I had every intention of flying to California to bring you back."

"You're saying this now," she said, shaking her head, "but in time you'll have a totally different outlook on things."

"Then we'll give it time to prove I meant everything I've sai—" But he stopped talking because his cell phone had rung. He checked the caller ID. It was his attorney. Talk about timing. "I've got to take this. Finish your breakfast. There's more on the stove. I'll be right back."

Andreas slipped out to his cabin and clicked on. "Yorgos?"

"I'm glad you picked up."

"Tell me you've got good news."

"I wish I did." Andreas grimaced. "Lia's attorney has counter-petitioned the judge for full custody of Ari. She's accusing you of a liaison with Kyria Perkins, who stayed in your hotel room with you on visitation."

"We both know she had her own hotel room, Yorgos."

"Of course. I provided the proof, but that's not the key issue."

He could feel his blood boil. "Go ahead and tell me."

"The counter-petition includes the following points in so many words—you're not emotionally stable this soon after your separation to be a good father. She's demanding a full psychological investigation. Secondly, she fears that you and your American lover will leave the country with Ari and not return, placing him in extreme jeopardy."

Andreas leaned against the wall while he calmed down. "Lia thinks I'll cave and ask her to come back, but she's just made her fatal mistake. When we hang up, I want you to call her attorney and tell him I'll be contacting the birth father today. He knows what this will mean to her. It could change everything."

"You're right. Consider it done."

"Thanks, Yorgos."

He hung up and went back to the kitchen. Zoe

had finished eating and was doing the dishes when she saw him.

"Is everything all right?"

"That was my attorney on the phone."

"I thought so."

"Lia is trying to hold things up, so I'm going ahead with my plans to tell Norville he has a son."

He saw that anxious look enter her eyes again. "Before you do anything, I need to answer your question about how to approach Norville."

Andreas had been waiting. "I'm all ears."

"You're such an honest and straightforward person, why don't you simply approach him at his office like you would any business contact? I can't see you doing it any other way. I guess it's my sense of you."

Relieved she'd finally given him one of the answers he'd wanted, he sat back down and pulled out his phone.

"Would you mind if I made the call right now? It's ten thirty here, which means nine thirty there. If he's not at work, I'll leave my number."

"Are you sure about this?"

"After the discussions we've had, I've never been more convinced it's the right thing to do."

She stood up. "I'll give you some privacy."

"I'd rather you stayed with me. Do you mind?"

"No," she answered in a quiet voice and sat back down on her chair.

"I've already preprogrammed Norville's realty office number the private detective gave me. It's the only number he could find." Without hesitation he pressed the digit.

After four rings, a male voice answered in French. *"Oui?"*

Andreas thought it odd the person didn't reply with the name of the business. Speaking in French, he said, "I'd like to speak to Guion Norville."

The man on the other end took a breath Andreas could hear. "Who's calling?"

"Andreas Gavras, from Patras, Greece. Is he available?"

After a long wait, "I'm afraid not."

He frowned. "Can he be reached at another

number? If not, would you ask him to call my number? It's of extreme urgency that I talk to him."

"Monsieur Norville is no longer available."

Andreas heard the click. The man had just hung up on him. He darted Zoe a puzzled glance and explained what had happened.

"Do you think he answered and pretended to be someone else when he found out who you were?"

"I'm not sure."

"Maybe he doesn't work there anymore. Didn't you say he dabbled in other businesses?"

"Yes."

"Maybe he has hired someone to answer the phone."

"Then again it's possible he's in financial trouble. But I can't imagine him hiding from creditors unless his family has cut off his money. There's only one solution. I'm going to call the detective agency right now and get to the bottom of it."

Andreas got back on the phone and asked to

speak to Gus. In another minute he came on the line.

"Andreas?"

"Gus? I just had a strange conversation with someone at that realty number you gave me for Guion Norville." He told him the gist of it.

"That is odd. It's the only phone number I have for him. I haven't yet found his wife's. To my knowledge the name Norville Realty is still on the front door."

"I need the address."

"Here it is. In the meantime I'll make more inquiries and get back to you if I find out any new information."

"Thanks, Gus."

"What did he say?" Zoe asked after he hung up the phone.

"He's perplexed, too. After we get back to Patras tonight, I'll leave for Nice first thing in the morning and find him. Since this is all I can do for now, let's go up on deck. We might see some dolphins."

Andreas left the galley first. He'd asked her to go to France with him, but didn't hold out hope.

To his surprise she followed right behind him. He reached for another life jacket and handed it to her. The other one had to be in her cabin. After she put it on, she walked over to the side to look out at the water. "I can't get over it. Another sunny, beautiful Grecian day."

He found his binoculars to help her search, but couldn't refrain from admiring her legs. Everything about her appealed to him.

"This is the experience of a lifetime. Oh— look! Two of them, jumping together!"

"The dolphins love the sun, too. If you'll notice, their beaks are short. They're the common dolphins. We might see some striped ones later."

For a half hour they watched at least six of them cavorting. Zoe made excited noises and used her cell phone to take pictures. When the activity stopped, she sat down next to him on the banquette and handed him the binoculars.

"That was spectacular. Thank you. I never expected to see a sight like that."

"You can see it most days if you catch them at the right time."

"Especially if you're out in a boat like this with a skipper who knows where to look."

He chuckled. "I'll take us for a ride. We might spot more. Since you expressed a desire to see the sea salt plant, I'll head farther along the coast and show you where it's located." He walked over to the bridge and raised the anchor. "Later we'll come back and swim. How does that sound?"

"What do *you* think?"

"I think you have an extraordinary nature that sees the best in everything. You're very easy company, Zoe. I thought it from the moment of the taxi accident. Your only concern was for the driver. If you've ever complained about anything, I haven't heard it."

She smiled. "There's a lot you don't know about me, but thank you."

After going ashore in Messolonghi for lunch,

Andreas drove her to the huge, modern sea salt plant in a rental car. Over the years he'd had renovations made.

"Your parents must have been so proud of your accomplishments running the hotel business and all this, too. I wish I could have met them."

"They would have loved you. Mother especially would have been delighted to know that you're an expert on Lord Byron, and teach literature at UCLA. It might interest you to know she was a whiz at math before she married my father.

"Like you she taught it as a graduate student at the University of Patras for several years. Later on she worked for a company that did computational math and informatics."

"It *might* interest me?" Zoe blurted. "How come it's taken until now for you to tell me? No wonder your parents gave birth to one of the most successful men in Greece."

Deep laughter rolled out of him.

"Laugh all you want, but your modesty is

one of your most admirable traits, Andreas. I'm thrilled to know about your mother's background and thrilled to be shown around your world."

"She was disappointed she couldn't have more children and found her work satisfying."

"How did your father feel about it?"

"He encouraged her. She was easy to get along with, too. They made a good team, better than most because they understood each other's needs."

"You've just described what went wrong in the marriage of my adoptive parents. Nancy got so caught up in children, I'm pretty sure Bob couldn't take it any longer. What drove her drove him away in the end. But both of them sacrificed a lot to raise me and the other kids. For that I'll always be grateful."

"Amen," Andreas declared before driving them to the dock where he left the car to be picked up. "On our way back to the cove, I'll pull you waterskiing if you'd like."

"Maybe another time. It's too soon after that

incredible lunch. Thank you for suggesting it, though." He was doing everything possible to make this trip unforgettable, but she knew he was brooding over a situation that was impacting his entire life.

Once in the boat she put on her life jacket. "Andreas—you've been wonderful to me, but I'd rather we returned to Patras now and swam another time. With the trip to France coming up in the morning, I know you need to go by your office and have a lot to do first."

He studied her intently. "Why this sudden change?"

"Not sudden, but that phone call from your attorney changed the stakes, and I'm one of the reasons why. Lia saw me with you and it made her livid because she wants you back and thinks I'm standing in her way."

"It's past time she sees that I'm moving on."

"But I can tell you're preoccupied even though you hide it well. You wouldn't be human if you weren't worrying about Ari's birth father. What will be his reaction to meeting you? What kind of a man is he? Most of all, what kind of a father will he make if he wants to be one to Ari."

He pulled her close and kissed her until she was dizzy with longing. "The researcher in you constantly seeking for more truth has given you superhuman insights. At this point I don't know how I functioned until you came into my life."

Zoe hid her face against his shoulder. "I don't know how you can say that."

Andreas kissed her hair. "Because it's true. To be honest, it's going to be hard flying to Nice without you. I'm not sure how long I'll be gone. The fear that you'll decide to leave in order to uncomplicate things for me never leaves my mind."

Zoe realized that this strong, amazing man was admitting his vulnerability to her. She wondered if anyone had ever seen this side of him. The revelation broke her down.

"You shouldn't have to worry about anything on a mission this earthshaking. If it's what you really want, I'll go with you to Nice, Andreas." Zoe hugged him, hoping she wasn't making another big mistake. The first was going to Athens with him, giving Lia ammunition to use against him.

He crushed her tighter, muttering something in Greek against her forehead that sounded heartfelt. "Now I know everything's going to be all right."

She wished she did, but he was going into a situation with no guarantees. When she thought of all the help he'd given her while she'd been doing research, she couldn't turn him down when she loved him so desperately.

Once he let her go, she sat down on the banquette and they sped back to the port where he'd left his car. Though she saw more dolphins, her mind was on his ex-wife. Lia had entered into her marriage concealing a lie and the guilt had lost her Andreas's love even before the truth came out. Still, Zoe could tell Lia's love for her son was total.

It pained Zoe that she was now the other woman in Lia's eyes. The volatile situation had become a triangle she hadn't wanted any part of. But fate had brought her and Andreas together under the most innocent circumstances. The moment he'd told her he was separated with a child, she should have stopped seeing him.

Nancy would have told Zoe not to get entangled. *Find a man without baggage.*

However, life didn't work that way. Zoe's heart had a mind and will of its own. When Andreas had come over to the taxi to see if she was hurt, it was as if she'd been instantly melded to him. It was more than physical attraction. She'd felt a connection she couldn't explain and knew would never go away.

Until he found Ari's birth father and all the visitation issues were settled in court, Zoe would stand by him while he did the right thing for his son. She loved him too much to do anything else. But as far as their future was concerned, she would leave Greece so Lia couldn't keep on using her as a weapon against Andreas.

Zoe could hear his argument that Lia would fight him as long as any woman was in his life. She feared that was true. Andreas's life would never be an easy one. A lot of divorced couples had troubles for years where financial fortunes and children were involved.

Once visitation had been permanently resolved, he could let go of the past and start living out the life destiny intended for him. Zoe didn't see herself as a part of it, only a means to different ends for both of them.

She'd met a man a breed apart from other men. She could never have imagined it in her dreams. He'd told her he was in love with her. She knew he'd meant it for the present and she'd been reveling in it from the beginning.

But she didn't trust first love feelings from a man who wasn't divorced yet, who hadn't yet explored all the possibilities for romantic involvement still awaiting him. At thirty-one years of age, he had years of living ahead of him filled with beautiful, remarkable women of his own country who would do anything to be loved by him. At least then, Lia wouldn't worry that he would leave Greece with his American lover and Ari.

"What's going on in your mind to put such a fierce expression on your face?"

Zoe had been so deep in thought she hadn't realized they'd reached the port and pulled into his private slip.

"Divorce can be so ugly, even if it's necessary."

"Don't worry, Zoe. This will pass."

"I don't know how you hold it all together."

He shut off the engine. "You haven't been listening. You're the reason I'm able to handle everything. Maybe the time will come when you'll believe me."

She wanted to believe it now, but she was afraid. "I'll go below to get my things."

"I'll come with you."

Mindful of his rock-hard body right behind her, she gathered her bag and cosmetics. They met on the dock. He brought the flowers with him. After he tied up the boat, they walked to his car and left for the city. But he took a different route that led to Kalamaki, the exclusive area of Patras she'd heard of but had never been to.

"Where are we going?"

"To my villa. I'd like you to see where I live."

"No, Andreas. Lia saw me in your hotel suite in Athens. She has people watching you, but so far you haven't taken me to the home she shared with you and Ari. It's too personal. She's just waiting to get something else on you that will look damning to the judge. I want to stay out of this as much as possible until he renders a final decision."

Zoe thought he hadn't been listening to her until he made a turn midblock and headed back to the freeway, taking them into the center. With a population of over two hundred and sixty thousand, Patras was the third-largest city in Greece.

"Please don't think I'd rather not see it. You know I do, but it's not wise. I'm already a stumbling block for you. Let's not make it any worse."

She noticed he gripped the steering wheel

tighter. "I'll take you to your apartment right now and come by for you at six in the morning."

With the tension thick between them, he parked in front of her flat and carried in her bag and flowers. This time he walked all the way inside to put the arrangement on the coffee table.

Zoe felt terrible. "Andreas? Tell me you understand."

His black eyes flashed fire before he put his hands on her shoulders. "I understand a lot more than you think I do. Lia has tried to get in my head, but instead she has gotten in yours. I'm too thankful you're going to Nice with me to fight that right now."

Before she could take a breath, his head descended and his mouth devoured hers until she was weaving in his arms. She let out a protesting moan when he lifted his lips from hers. "I love you, Zoe, and I'll keep repeating it until you feel it in the very depths of *your* DNA."

He left the flat so fast, she clung to the nearest chair so she wouldn't collapse. *Andreas*, her heart cried.

* * *

Once in the car, Andreas headed straight for his office. If he hadn't left Zoe's flat when he did, no telling if he would ever leave. Much as he'd wanted to take her home with him, she wouldn't have been comfortable. Her guilt was too great for having been named as part of the reason Lia was being vindictive.

The judge couldn't make a definitive ruling soon enough for Andreas. He was counting the hours. After he reached the office, he placed another call to Gus and had to leave a message. While he waited for a response, he dug into the paperwork piled up on his desk requiring signatures.

The Gavras House Hotel board of directors meeting was scheduled for Thursday at 9:00 a.m. Today was Tuesday. That gave him tomorrow to find Guion Norville and talk to him.

He made a call to his grandparents to check on them. They wanted to see Ari. Andreas told them he was working on redoing his visitation. It wouldn't be long before his son was spending a whole week at a time with him in Patras. Then he let his grandfather know about the board meeting. The second they hung up, Gus phoned him.

"Andreas?"

"Thanks for getting back to me tonight, Gus. I'm leaving for Nice at six in the morning. Is there anything else you've learned?"

"I just found out he has a cousin living in Nice, Philippe Norville, who owns a Peugeot dealership. If all else fails, you might try him."

Andreas wrote down the address. "You've been a great help, Gus. I'm putting a check in the mail to you tonight."

"Thank you. Let me know if you make contact with Norville."

"I will."

After they hung up, he phoned Yorgos to let him know he was headed for Nice in the morning. "Once I've made contact with Guion Norville, I'll call to let you know the situation. If he has an attorney, I'll give him your information."

"Good luck, Andreas."

He rang off and headed for his villa. Zoe had agreed to go with him tomorrow. She'd become necessary to his existence. With her he knew he could handle anything that came along in life.

But the more he thought about it, the more he wondered if she had deeper feelings for him than she'd been letting on. She still hadn't said the words he was desperate to hear. If she only understood how deep his love was for her.

After the two-hour flight, the Gavras jet landed in Nice at 9:00 a.m. under semicloudy skies. Andreas helped Zoe down the steps to the limo waiting for them and gave the driver instructions where to go.

"There's a real change in temperature from Patras," Zoe remarked as Andreas slid in next to her and grasped her hand. She'd worn a summery café au lait suit with short sleeves and a white blouse. He loved her dress sense. She looked breathtaking in anything, and the strawberry fragrance from her hair brought his senses alive.

"It's seventy-five degrees this morning, but it'll warm up a little." He studied her profile. "Are you all right? You've been quieter than usual."

Zoe turned to him. "I was going to ask you the same question. I bet you didn't get any sleep last night."

"You're wrong." He kissed her beautiful mouth. "Knowing you would be with me today helped me get my first sound sleep in a long time."

She squeezed his hand tighter. "I admire your strength, Andreas...and your goodness," she whispered.

"What do you mean?"

"I know I've said this before, but not everyone would be prepared to make this sacrifice." He heard a tremor in her voice. "Instead of hiding behind a secret for the rest of your life, you're prepared to do anything for your son." Tears welled in those glorious blue eyes. "He's so blessed to have a father like you."

Andreas's throat swelled with emotion.

"That's how I've felt since you came into my life. Your incredible story helped me understand that Guion Norville has to know the truth.

"In the beginning I was struggling with the thought of telling him because I couldn't bear the thought of losing Ari. But after meeting you and our talks, I knew I had to be fair to Guion. One day Ari will have to be told, too. Without you, I don't believe I would ever have seen things as clearly. I'm the one who's thankful."

The limo took them alongside the Promenade des Anglais lined with varieties of palms next to the beach. "What a magnificent shoreline, Andreas. I can see why this part of the French Riviera attracts people in droves."

"It has a unique ambience all its own. If Norville wants to know Ari and have a relationship with him, then this city will play an important part in his life."

Andreas had told himself over and over again that he would be able to handle it. But as he took in the famous Mediterranean scenery with its mixture of French and Italian architecture, he experienced pain that one day Ari would learn to love this city through Guion's eyes. The two of them would have experiences no one else would share. Andreas wouldn't be a part of it.

The hand he'd been holding pressed his hard. He could swear Zoe knew what was going through his mind. It was as if she'd just said, *This isn't about you. It's about your son, who will thank you for this one day.*

"Where are we going first, Andreas?"

"To his realty office. It's coming up here on Boulevard Napoleon III."

"When we get there, I plan to stay in the limo and wait for you."

He knew she would say that. The fact that she'd come with him at all was more than he could have wished for.

"The crowds are big everywhere. Earlier I told the driver to find a parking space and wait for my phone call." In another minute they pulled up in front of the address Gus had given him and came to a stop.

Zoe drew in a breath before giving him a kiss on the jaw. "All my hopes go with you."

"That's what is helping me." He brushed her lips with his own before getting out of the limo.

Walking between two parked cars, he approached the entrance to Norville Riviera Realty on the corner. But before he even tried to open the door, he saw the sign reading Closed Permanently set in the glass. Andreas peered inside. All he saw was a folding chair and an empty desk.

He walked next door to the travel agency on the east. Several tourists were inside looking at brochures. A woman at the counter smiled at him. "Can I help you?"

"Could you tell me how long the Norville Realty company has been vacated?" he asked in French.

She acted surprised. "It has? I had no idea."

Was she telling the truth? "Did you know the owner?"

"No. I met the manager once maybe two months ago."

"Do you remember his name?"

"I'm sorry."

So was Andreas. He'd come to a dead end. "Thank you."

He left the agency and walked out to the street. To his surprise the limo driver came along in another minute. He walked around to tell him to go to the next address on the Rue Lamartine.

Zoe sat forward when he climbed in the back. Her face mirrored her anxiety. "That didn't take long."

Andreas caressed the side of her cheek as the limo merged with the traffic. "There was a sign in the window that said Closed. The travel agent next door didn't know it had been vacated."

"I can't believe it. After all this, I'm so sorry."

"I'm not foiled yet. Gus gave me the address of his cousin Philippe Norville. He runs a car dealership here in Nice. I told the driver to take us there now."

She moistened her lips nervously. "If he's at his office, what will you say to him?"

"That I'm trying to find Guion."

"This Philippe might associate you with your sea salt company."

"I'll use my mother's middle name."

She blinked. "What was her last name?"

"Calista Valieri."

"That's lovely. So you'll be Kyrie Valieri. What will be your reason for looking for him?"

"I'll say that I was thinking of buying some investment property in Nice. I heard that Monsieur Guion Norville might be able to help me. But I couldn't reach him on the phone and discovered he'd moved his place of business. That's when I found the name Philippe Norville in the directory.

"Since the Norville name was prominent, I wondered if he was a relative who knew where I could find Monsieur Norville's new place of business. I thought I'd make inquiries before seeking out another Realtor." He cocked his head. "How does that sound to you?"

"I think it could work, but it's still taking a risk because you're trying to spare Norville and yourself any hint of scandal. Andreas...what if I made the inquiry while you stayed in the limo?

"I'd say what you would have said, but I'd explain that I was looking for a time-share for me and some friends from California when we come on vacation to the Riviera. I'd tell him someone at the hotel told me Monsieur Norville handled that sort of business. Was there a number where I could reach him?"

Zoe was phenomenal, but he shook his head. "I can't allow you to get any more involved in my problem."

"I've come this far. He would never associate me with you. It's worth a try and you won't have to lie."

The light in her eyes had him mesmerized. "I'll never be able to repay you."

"You know that's not what I'm after. I'm pretending that I'm in search of finding my own father. Since I can't do that, let me help you. It will mean a lot to me."

Those particular words got to him like nothing else could have done. Andreas pulled her into his arms and clung to her until the limo slowed to a stop in the parking lot of the dealership. He kissed her thoroughly, holding her tight. "I still can't let you do this."

"Don't you know I want to? We have to do whatever it takes. If he's there, this should go quickly." With another kiss, she slid over to the door and got out.

"Zoe?"

"It's going to be all right. Trust me."

He realized he had to. "I'll be right here," he assured her.

With a pounding heart, Andreas, along with the men milling around the dealership, watched the stunning dark blonde woman disappear inside the main doors. Though Zoe was a modern-day woman, she was a warrior and he was in awe of her.

CHAPTER EIGHT

THE SECOND ZOE walked inside, an attractive salesman dressed in light blue suit with brown hair and eyes came right up to her. *"Puis-je vous aider, mademoiselle?"*

"Do you speak English?"

"Ah. *Americaine.*" He smiled. "I'll do my best."

He had that French charm, reminding her a little of Raoul Decorvet. His best English was pretty good, too. "Would it be possible to see Monsieur Philippe Norwood, the owner?"

The man acted surprised. "You know him?"

"No, but I'm hoping he can help me."

"He went to lunch, but should return any minute. Maybe there's something I can do for you while you're waiting. I'll be happy to show you our latest models."

"Thank you, but I'd prefer to speak to him."

"*Bien sur.* I'll walk back to his office. He might be here already. May I give him your name?"

"Yes. It's Zoe Perkins."

"Please take a seat over here." He handed her a brochure. "I'll be right back."

She sat down, knowing Andreas had to be in his own private agony while he waited for her. Zoe looked around. Other salesmen were helping customers. This dealership obviously did well. She was impressed with the man who'd greeted her. He had a professionalism and wasn't pushy. If she'd wanted to buy a car, she wouldn't have minded his help.

"Mademoiselle Perkins?" She lifted her head. "Please come with me. Monsieur Norville has returned and will see you now."

Her pulse sped up. Maybe now she'd get an answer for Andreas. "Thank you." Zoe put the brochure on the chair next to her and followed the salesman around a corner and down a hall to the owner's office. The substantial older man standing behind the desk invited her to sit down.

"What can I do for you?"

"I've taken a chance coming to you and am probably wasting your time. I'm looking for a Monsieur Guion Norville who owns a realty company here in Nice. Someone at the hotel where I'm staying recommended him. I was hoping he would help me to invest in a time-share for me and my friend who is waiting for me in the parking lot.

"But when I went there this morning, it had a closed sign in the window. If he moved his business to a different location, I'd like to know where. The travel agency next door couldn't help me. Then I saw your name in the directory. Before I go to another Realtor, I thought I would ask you if you've heard of him since you have the same last name."

He sat forward and put his hands flat on the desk. "You just met him." Zoe almost had a heart attack. "He happens to be my cousin. I'll go find him and ask him to come back in."

The moment he left his office, Zoe phoned Andreas, who answered after the first ring. "Zoe? What's happening?"

"Guion is here," she whispered. "He greeted me at the door and is obviously working for Philippe."

"I can't believe it." Andreas had to be in shock. So was she.

"Gus gave you a perfect lead. I met his cousin, who has gone to find Guion and bring him back to his office. Whatever happens, don't be surprised." She hung up because she heard footsteps coming down the hall.

Guion walked in and shut the door so they were alone. His eyes played over her with a hint of suspicion. "This *is* a surprise. No one has come looking for me since I got out of the realty business. Why are you really looking for me? I know we've never met or I would have remembered you."

The game was up. Zoe got to her feet. "You're right. I'm not the person who wants to talk to you. But since you're working, I'll tell him to come another time."

"Him?"

"My friend. He's waiting for me in the parking lot."

"In that case I'll accompany you since you've aroused my curiosity."

Uh-oh. This was it. Her heart pounded so hard, it was unhealthy. With fingers crossed, she left the office with him and they walked out of the building to the waiting limo.

Andreas had been lounging against the rear door with his arms crossed. When he saw them coming, he straightened. In a silky tan sport shirt and white pants, and his raven-black hair disheveled by a slight Mediterranean breeze, Andreas took her breath. His fiery black eyes met hers, sending an unspoken message of amazement.

Zoe loved him so intensely, she had to get hold of her emotions before turning to the other man. "Monsieur Norwood, I'd like you to meet Andreas Gavras."

Guion's hands came out of his pockets, and his brows lifted. "*The* Andreas Gavras who's not only CEO of Gavras House Hotels, but the Gavras Sea Salt Company?" Andreas nodded. "Your name is well-known. Why would you want to talk to me? I haven't worked in my family's shipping business for many years."

From his reaction, she saw no indication of alarm. Zoe could almost believe Guion truly didn't know Lia had been engaged to Andreas when they'd made love, or that there'd been consequences.

How hard this had to be for Andreas, and in another minute for both men who were actually the same height. Guion was probably thirty-five. Now that she'd had a chance to meet him in person, she could see he'd bequeathed his rangier build to Ari. Genes didn't lie.

She was sure Andreas was noticing all this and much more when he said, "I've come for one reason only. To let you know you have a sixteen-and-a-half-month-old son named Ari. It's your God-given right to know you have a child with Lia Pappas, as she was before we married, but what you choose to do with this information is your business alone."

Even in the partial sunlight Zoe thought Guion lost some color.

Zoe touched Andreas's arm. "It's getting busy out here," she said in an aside. "Someone could hear us."

Andreas eyed the other man, who'd gone quite still. "Shall we talk in the limo?"

Guion nodded and climbed inside. He sat opposite her and Andreas. "Why did Lia send *you* to tell me?"

"She didn't. This was all my idea. She never wanted you to know and hoped neither you nor I would ever find out the truth. What she hadn't counted on was Ari having to undergo an operation from a ruptured intestine earlier this year. He needed blood. That's when I found out I wasn't his father, so I filed for divorce."

A pain-filled epithet escaped Guion's lips.

"I confronted Lia with her lie. Apparently she

spent the night with you without telling you we were engaged."

"She didn't say a word. Neither did her friend. I didn't know she was engaged to you, I swear it."

"I believe you," Andreas stated. "But she's terrified that this will cause a devastating scandal for all families concerned if it comes out. No one wants that."

Guion moaned.

"I've come to you for one reason. Do you want to be a father to Ari and share in visitation? If you do, Lia lives with her parents in Athens. You would have to travel there. It's what I have to do so I can be with Ari. He's the light of my life."

His love for his boy caused Zoe's eyelids to smart.

The man's hands went to his face. "My first wife has remarried, but we have a daughter together named Cecile. I send child support and try to see her. At present I'm separated from my second wife, but it's not what I want.

"I've lost family money trying to start other businesses. My cousin Philippe is helping me out right now so I can get back together with Vivige and my son Dominic. But if I tell her the truth, that I was drunk that weekend in Athens with friends who talked me into going to a party on the Palaskas yacht, she'll never take me back. It didn't mean anything. That night was a complete blur and I've despised myself for what I did, but it's too late."

"If you love her, then you need to convince her." Zoe loved Andreas for saying that.

"I do, but she'll never accept my having been unfaithful and producing another child that isn't ours."

Zoe's eyes fused with Andreas's. They could both see the man had to be overwhelmed with guilt and problems.

Guion's lined face lifted. "Are you saying no one knows about this?"

Andreas shook his head. "Eliana Palaskas is Lia's best friend and has probably figured it out by now. My grandparents know, and Zoe knows, plus my attorney and Lia's."

"But not Lia's parents?"

"No. You have my word no one else from my world will ever know if you decide not to claim him. It's entirely up to you."

"I can't think right now."

"I understand," Andreas said with compassion. "I have pictures of Ari from two days ago on my cell phone. Would you like to see him?"

He shook his head. "You've been his father all this time. It would be best if I never see him and he never finds out."

"I can't promise that, Guion. One day Ari might find out by accident, the way I did because of the wrong blood type. I intend to tell him when he's ready. If you decide you want no contact ever, then he'll be told. I'd advise you to talk this over with an attorney and get back to mine. Is there anyone you can confide in about this? Someone you trust?"

"Philippe always has my back."

Andreas nodded. "That's good. Tell you what.

We're going to fly back to Patras tonight. I'll give you my attorney's card. When or if you want to get in touch with me, call him and he'll arrange it. I won't be coming to Nice again or bothering you in any way."

"You're an amazing man, Gavras."

How many times had Zoe said the same thing about Andreas? "Monsieur Norville? I hope you won't mind if I say something here. I never knew my parents or their names or their backgrounds. Nothing. I was raised in two foster families until I turned eighteen. I'd give anything on earth to know even the slightest detail about either of my real parents.

"Your birth son Ari is so lucky because you are alive and could be reached if it's what he wants one day. Should you decide not to acknowledge him ever, would you at least consider leaving the situation open legally in case he'd just like to see you one time? Talk to you? Write to you? Get a sense of his genetic makeup? Anything?"

He looked at her for a minute. "I'm sorry you never knew your parents."

"If that's true, then please consider it for his sake."

"I'll think about what you said." He turned to Andreas. "I need to get back to work."

Andreas put out his hand. After a slight hesitation, Guion shook it and climbed out of the limo. Before he walked away, he looked at Zoe. "You're amazing, too."

After he walked back in the building, Andreas clutched her in his arms, burying his face in her hair. "You're beyond awesome, Zoe. Because of you, I was able to talk to him without raising suspicions. You're an angel who made all this possible and I'm in your debt forever."

She clung to him, knowing what all this meant to him. "I feel for him, Andreas. I admire you so much for showing him the compassion you did. There's no one to match you." Zoe kissed the side of his neck, loving this man and his humanity.

He pulled out his phone. "I'm going to call

Yorgos right now and tell him what's happening. I'll put it on speaker. Then I want to devote the rest of this day to you. I thought we'd drive over to the old town.

"There's a restaurant in a basement with walls of stone and brick. They restored some cellars and serve delicious cheese fondue. After that we'll walk around and visit some Impressionist museums if you'd like."

"I'd love to see the Matisse."

"We'll do it." He kissed her thoroughly before calling his attorney.

"Yorgos? I have news! I caught up with Norville and the truth is out." Zoe noticed how his eyes gleamed in relief.

"Congratulations. This should change things with Lia. I'll call her attorney the second we're off the phone," Yorgos replied.

"When Lia hears this, I have to hope she reconsiders how she's handling visitation. Norville isn't sure what he wants to do yet. I gave him your card to give to his attorney. I told him I won't be in contact with him again. This was it. Just so you know, I'll be back in Patras to-night."

"Excellent. We'll stay in close touch."

Andreas hung up and clasped her to him again. Zoe knew an almost unbearable weight had been lifted from him and she hugged him back. Her heart was lighter, too. She could only hope that if Guion didn't want anything to do with Ari, he would at least allow his son to see him one day or talk to him.

The chauffeur drove them across Nice to the old town past French and Italian architecture that made the city so charming. Two hours later they'd eaten fondue and he'd introduced her to *tentura*, a citrus wine made in Patras since the 1500s that was divine.

Later they wandered through the narrow streets and alleys before the limo drove them to the seventeenth-century villa where the Matisse collection was housed.

She clung to Andreas's arm. "If I had to be locked up in one place for days on end, I'd choose to be here. The way Matisse painted flowers, or a woman lying on a bed, or a scene out of a window, his use of color, it all delights me. Do you have a favorite Impressionist painter?"

"Van Gogh speaks to me."

"I love a lot of his paintings, too. I also love the sculptures of Rodin, especially *The Kiss* and *Eternal Springtime.*"

His eyes danced. "Those are two of my favorites, as you can imagine."

She blushed. "Of course I've only seen those in pictures. One day I'll get to Paris and see the real thing. What Greek artists do you like?" It was time to change the subject.

"There's a sculpture of Hermes carrying the infant Dionysus done by Praxiteles in the archaeological museum in Olympia. My parents took me there when I was ten or eleven. My mother said the baby reminded her of me. I didn't think about it again until Ari's operation. Oddly enough the infant reminded me of him. Mother bought a postcard I still have."

"That's something I'd like to see."

"I'll show it to you when we get home."

"Speaking of home, we'd better leave for the airport, Andreas. I've kept you walking around in here for hours. I know you're anxious to get back."

"If I'm anxious, it's so we can be strictly alone."

There was nothing Zoe desired more, but Andreas wasn't out of the woods yet where Lia was concerned. As they walked out of the elegant villa to the waiting limo, she knew they were getting to the point of no return.

If after all this Lia still proved to be difficult, even knowing her lie had been exposed to Guion, then Zoe needed to leave for California. She absolutely refused to be the reason he couldn't have the visitation he'd petitioned for.

They boarded the Gavras private jet and ate dinner. Andreas made some business calls to his assistant and one of his uncles. When they arrived in Patras, Andreas walked her to his car. But on the way into the city, he followed a freeway sign that led to an area called Kalamaki. Zoe hadn't been there but knew it was an exclusive neighborhood of the city.

"I thought you were taking me to my apartment."

"I want you with me tonight. I'm taking you to my villa."

She sucked in her breath. "No, Andreas. I've told you this before. Much as I'd like to see where you live, I don't dare. Lia could have people watching. All she'd need is another picture of you and me together walking into the house where she lived with you, and it would inflame her more. Your visitation petition needs to be ruled on first."

When she saw Andreas grip the steering wheel tighter, Zoe knew she'd upset what had been a beautiful afternoon and evening. In the next block he made a U-turn and they headed back to the freeway that would take them into the city.

"I'd hoped to leave you at the villa where you could laze and swim in the pool while I'm at my board meeting tomorrow. Instead when I come by to pick you up after it's over, I'll discover you're not there."

"Andreas—" She'd really done some serious damage to his trust when she'd flown to Italy without preparing him. "I'm not leaving Patras. While you're busy at your meeting, I'll do some errands. Please don't be upset."

"You don't seem to understand. I don't want you out of my sight."

She closed her eyes tightly. "I love every minute we're together, too, but while you're in this visitation battle, we have to be careful. What if something goes wrong and it's all my fault?"

He pulled up in front of her apartment and turned off the engine. "Look at me, Zoe." She turned to him. "How could you possibly be to blame for anything? Lia can't deprive me of being with my son. Her tactics won't hold up. In another few days it will all be settled."

"I want to believe that, too, Andreas. That's why I'm going to say good-night to you now. Please stay in the car. There's probably some private detective working for her who's been lurking around here. Let's not give that person any more incriminating evidence than they already have. I'll run in my flat alone." She started to get out.

"Wait—"

"No," she insisted firmly. "It's better if I go in alone. I'll be waiting for your call tomorrow. Go home and get the sleep you need so you can be at your best during the meeting." She fought not to tear up. "Being with you today was the highlight of my entire life. I'll never forget it."

He called her name, but she shut the door and ran to her flat before she broke down and begged him to come in with her. This situation couldn't go on much longer.

Her body ached for him. She was so in love, she hurt with the pain of it. Zoe knew he loved her and was in pain, too, but it was a different level of love than the one he had for his son. As he'd told Guion, Ari was his life, and that life was more important than what she and Andreas had together.

He'd said it would be a few more days and everything would be settled, implying that they could then be together without worry. But she had deep reservations on that score. Zoe wasn't blind. Lia hadn't given up on Andreas and was fighting to regain the love he'd once felt for her.

Zoe took off her clothes to shower and wash her hair. Once she'd gotten ready for bed and dried it, she climbed under the covers, praying sleep would come. For once she didn't feel like talking to anyone about this. No one could solve this problem.

Andreas's wife had felt threatened to see Zoe in his hotel room in Athens. If she hadn't gone with him… But it did no good to go over it in her mind.

Zoe turned over on her stomach, burying her face in the pillow. Tears started to trickle out of her eyes until she began sobbing. Though she'd told Andreas she wouldn't leave, she'd only meant that she'd be here for him tomorrow.

Zoe's gut feeling was that in the end, Guion wouldn't want visitation rights and would put it in writing in order to save his marriage. As for her and Andreas, she intended to tell him goodbye for now. One day he'd obtain his divorce. Then they could be together because he'd be a free man. That's what she intended to tell Andreas before oblivion took over.

CHAPTER NINE

As soon as the Thursday board of directors meeting had come to an end, Andreas hugged his grandfather, then hurried out to the parking lot and got in his car. It was noon. Zoe had to be wondering what was taking so long.

When he heard his phone ring, he checked the caller ID and was surprised to see that his house-keeper was on the other end. She came to the villa a few hours every day to keep things up.

He clicked on. "Gaia?"

"Please excuse me for disturbing you, Kyrie. I know you're in a meeting, but I'm sure you'll want to be told about this."

"That's no problem. It's over. What's wrong? You sound distressed."

"Kyria Gavras just arrived at the villa in a taxi with the little one."

Andreas's mind reeled. Lia had flown here with Ari? Obviously the news that he'd met with Guion Norville had caused her to do something unprecedented.

"I let her in because I didn't know what else to do. She went straight to Ari's bedroom."

"It's all right, Gaia. Thank you for telling me. I'll be home in ten minutes."

He'd been headed for the apartment, but changed directions. En route to the villa he phoned Zoe.

"Andreas—are you still in the meeting?"

"It's finally over and I was on my way to the bedsitter, but something else came up. My housekeeper just phoned to tell me Lia has arrived at the villa with Ari."

"You're kidding!"

"Our visit to Nice must have shaken her."

"That's good news, don't you think? If she's here to talk, maybe you can get everything straightened out and not have to go through your attorneys. Don't worry about me. I'll grab a bite of lunch in town and wait for your call."

He loved Zoe so intensely, he was going to lose his mind if they couldn't be together permanently before long. "I swear I'll get back to you as soon as I can. I couldn't live without you." His voice shook. "Remember that."

He hung up and broke the fifty-mile-an-hour speed limit to get back to the villa. Once he'd pulled in the circular drive and let himself in the front entrance, he raced through to Ari's bedroom.

Looking on from the doorway, he saw Lia seated on the double bed watching their son, who was asleep in his crib. She'd pulled out his box of little wooden trains. He could see them lined up. It was a familiar sight. The remembered scene brought a pang to Andreas's heart to see him back in his own room. It had seemed like forever.

Lia must have noticed Andreas because she suddenly stood up and walked into the hall with him. Her jaw grew taut. "Gaia didn't waste any time telling you I'd come."

"Shall we go out in the sunroom to talk?" he

suggested in a low voice. "If he wakes up, we'll be able to hear him." She followed him to the room that looked out over the garden and sat down on one of the couches. He preferred to stand. "If you'd let me know you were coming, I would have rescheduled the board meeting and been here to let you in."

"I didn't make up my mind about it until early this morning."

That sounded like Lia, who had an impulsive nature. How odd that he'd once loved this woman, but now he truly felt nothing for her.

"Why are you here, Lia?"

"My attorney told me you'd been to Nice. I want to know what Guion said he was going to do. I'd rather hear it from you than through our attorneys. I'll need to prepare my parents if the worst has happened."

Lia was more frightened of their reaction to her lie than anything else. She needed their backing to survive.

"He's separated from his second wife. However, it's my opinion he wants to preserve his second marriage and won't ask for visitation rights."

"That means my parents might never have to know," she murmured.

"You're right. Guion already has two children by different wives. But I suppose he could change his mind before he signs any legal document. We'll just have to wait and see."

Her features looked drawn. "What are your plans?"

"Certainly not to fly to the United States and take Ari with me. If you thought I could do that to the mother of our son, then you never did know the real me."

"Yes I did." Her voice broke. "I only said those things because I was hurt you found someone else so fast."

"It wasn't fast, Lia. I found you first, the only woman I ever asked to marry me. I planned to make a whole life with you. But you shut me out the moment you slept with Guion. We were estranged from that moment before we ever took our vows."

"I told you it never meant anything." He believed her. Like Guion, she'd been drinking heavily, too.

"It did to me. After talking to Norville, I believe he's as guilt ridden because of that night as you are. It's my guess that guilt over your infidelity ruined our marriage and his. What's your excuse for calling me unstable and demanding I be denied visitation while I undergo psychiatric evaluation?"

She averted her eyes. "My attorney came up with that idea to scare you so you'd give up Kyria Perkins. He knows I want to get back together with you."

"But you and I both know that's never going to happen. Have you moved into your villa?"

"I'm in the process." Andreas could tell she was trembling. "The renovations are almost done."

"That's good." Better than good.

"Are you going to marry her when the divorce is final?" she blurted.

"If she'll have me."

"Then you can't promise me you won't take Ari away."

Andreas took a deep breath. "If and when the time comes that she'll agree to be my wife, perhaps there'll come a day when we'll take a trip to Santa Monica, California, where she was raised by adoptive parents. But if we go, Ari will have to be older and able to handle a week's trip."

Her dark eyes widened. "She doesn't have real family?"

"They're real, just not blood. If we marry, our life will be here in Patras and you and I will go on working out visitation for the rest of Ari's life."

"How can you consider marrying someone like her?"

Andreas studied her hardened features. Much as he wanted to tell her it was none of her business, he couldn't. Naturally she was curious about the woman who might be helping raise Ari if Andreas had anything to do with it.

"If I started listing her virtues, I wouldn't

know where to stop. Zoe married early, but it only lasted a year and half because her husband was unfaithful to her. They didn't have children."

Lia turned away from him.

"She grew up a scholar and babysat for people to earn money. After winning awards and grants, she put herself through college and graduate school while working at the college bookstore. She's a professor at UCLA and was awarded a singular honor for her contribution to a film being made in Hollywood about Lord Byron while he was in Greece raising money to help fight the Turks."

Lia wheeled around. "How did you meet?"

"Quite literally by accident downtown. A truck ran into the taxi she was riding in. My limo was behind the truck and I called the paramedics. The last thing I expected that day was to meet another woman when our separation was only two days old. The two of us became friends first, pure and simple."

"I don't want to hear any more about this paragon," she broke in.

"The ball is in your court, Lia. Where do you want to go from here? Back to court? I'll undergo a psychiatric evaluation if that will satisfy you. What else must I do in order to have my visitation time with our son?"

He heard her sharp intake of breath. "You can have it starting right now for the next two days while I return to Athens. I'd like nothing better than to take Ari back with me right now, but because he's looking forward so much to seeing his *baba*, I'm not going to do that to him. Then you can fly him back on Sunday. I brought some of his things."

"Thank you for that, Lia."

"I'll tell my attorney we're waiting to hear from Guion. Everything hinges on him should he decide to exercise his rights and turn this into a public scandal. Until his attorney talks to mine, don't plan to come to Athens to see Ari or I'll have a restraining order filed against you."

"You can't do that."

"Watch me. You started this by insisting on telling Guion."

His insides froze because she couldn't see reason. Lia was terrified of the unknown with Ari's birth father in the picture. But she couldn't hold off Andreas for long.

"Did you hear me?"

"I did." He'd give it until Monday to see what developed on Norville's side before he asked Yorgos to take action.

"The limo driver is waiting to take me to the airport. Since Ari is asleep, I'll leave now. He'll be ready for juice and a snack when he wakes up."

He watched her disappear from the sunroom before he walked back down the hall to Ari's bedroom to check on him. His son was still crouched on his stomach in his white shorts and blue sailor top not moving, but he'd be awake before long. Taking advantage of the time, he phoned Zoe.

She picked up on the second ring. "Andreas?"

The anxiety in her voice told him she'd been worried. He needed to reassure her.

"Zoe? Lia has gone back to Athens and she left Ari with me until Sunday. I'll explain more later. Where are you?"

"Back at the apartment."

"Stay put. The limo will be by for you within ten minutes. He'll drive you here. Pack a bag and bring your swimsuit. When Ari wakes up from his nap, we'll go out to the pool."

"You're sure it will be all right?"

"Don't you trust me?"

"You *know* I do," she cried. "You must be overjoyed to see him!"

"Her arrival was a gift. I'll see you soon."

"He's so adorable." So was she. "I can't wait."

"You don't know the half of it."

Once they hung up, he called his limo driver and told him to pick up Zoe at her apartment. After that he phoned Yorgos to tell him what had happened with Lia.

"Let's just hope Norville acts quickly to bring this thing to an end, Andreas. If he doesn't, then your only choice is to inform Lia's parents of the truth. That'll be the end of the problems."

"I don't want to do that if I don't have to," Andreas said with a frown.

"That's your decency talking. We'll stay in close touch."

With both calls made, he hurried to his bedroom to change into his trunks and a T-shirt. Then he gathered towels and sunscreen for them.

Andreas was finally going to be alone with Zoe and his son in his own home. It had taken a long time to reach this point. One day soon he planned on getting his heart's desire. Being married to Zoe was all he could think about.

Zoe gasped softly as the limo drove along the seashore to Andreas's cream-colored villa with a red tiled roof, spread out over the property like a one-story exclusive resort. It overlooked a beach with a fantastic view of the entire bay of Patras. Everywhere her eyes wandered she saw olive and citrus trees with sweeping flower beds, grass and plants.

When the limo drove up the circular drive to the entrance where she saw his Mercedes parked, Andreas was waiting for her dressed to go swimming. Every time she saw him, it was like the first time and she struggled to catch her breath. He was beyond gorgeous in so many ways. How Lia could have been unfaithful to him made no sense to Zoe.

She assumed things had to be better with his ex-wife or she wouldn't have brought Ari to Patras and left him.

"Thank heaven you're here," he exclaimed after opening the door so she could get out. He reached for her bag and walked her inside the large foyer. You could see through to the swimming pool beyond the glass that formed the other side of the exquisite foyer filled with potted flowering plants.

"Oh, Andreas—" But those were the only two words that escaped before he crushed her in his arms and kissed the daylights out of her. She had no idea how long they tried to appease their hunger for each other. It didn't matter. This was where she wanted to be, in his home, in his strong arms. The ache to be loved by him was reaching its zenith.

He picked her up like a bride and carried her through part of the villa and down a hall to the nursery where Ari was sleeping. Smothering her mouth with another deep kiss, he followed her down on the double bed and began devouring her in earnest.

To lie next to him like this was ecstasy. While his powerful legs twined with her jean-clad limbs, she ran her hands through his black hair and kissed every feature, not able to get enough of him. Everywhere he touched her, he set her body on fire.

"I love you, Andreas. I love you so much it frightens me." The words poured out of her. She couldn't stop them.

"We have to get married, Zoe. I need you desperately." He stared down into her eyes. "Say you'll be my wife as soon as the divorce goes through."

Before she could answer him, they both heard Ari, who'd awakened without their knowledge and had gotten to his feet. He was shaking the crib railing and calling out "Baba!"

Andreas had to let her go and got up from the bed to reach for his son. "It's about time your mother brought you back so you could sleep in your own bedroom." He kissed him half a dozen times while Zoe sat up to watch the tender way he dealt with his boy.

Ari's cheeks were rosy from sleep. Andreas changed his diaper and put him in a darling swimming suit. Once dressed, he slipped sandals on him and carried him over to her. "Do you remember Zoe?"

His son didn't act interested or say her name. "I think he's disoriented to see me here."

"He'll get used to it since you're going to be an integral part of our lives."

Zoe hadn't said she'd marry him. He still hadn't told her where things really stood with

Lia, but just hearing Andreas say what he did sent a shiver of excitement through her.

"Come on. We left your bag in the foyer. Let's collect it and I'll show you to the guest bedroom where you can change."

His villa was a marvel of modern design; open, airy and full of light. The use of plants and paintings provided the color against the white walls. He showed her to the guest bedroom and waited while she put on her swimming suit and beach jacket in the en suite bathroom.

When she walked out, his lingering gaze on every part of her face and figure set her heart pounding. She followed him as they walked on fabulous Greek tiles to the immaculate kitchen that was a housewife's dream. Ari looked over Andreas's shoulder at her. "Are you beginning to remember me, Ari? I'm Zoe."

To her delight he finally said her name, producing happy laughter from Andreas. "We'll take out a drink and some snacks for him. Would you like a soda?"

"That sounds wonderful. I'll get it." She

reached in the fridge for a cola. "Do you want one, too?"

"Yes, please."

She trailed him through an alcove to some doors that opened onto more tiles surrounding the rectangular pool. It was a glittering blue in the afternoon sunlight.

"This has to be the reason you stay in such fabulous shape." Like a Greek god.

He grinned. "I don't know about fabulous, but I try to work out here every morning before I leave for work."

"What heaven!"

There were two umbrella tables with chairs and lounge chairs in a blue-and-white design that would always remind her she was in Greece. He'd already brought some towels and things out here, including a few water toys for Ari that included a little raft and a ball.

His daddy lowered him to the tiles and he ran to get the ball, which he immediately threw in the pool. They both laughed at his son's antics.

Zoe removed her white beach jacket. While

she'd been in Greece she'd bought a Grecian-designed swimming suit. It was a white one-piece that zipped up the front with some one-inch black stripes around the torso and hips. Being full-figured, she liked it for its modesty, plus the fact that she was crazy about black and white.

Again she felt Andreas's eyes play over her. This time it made her cheeks go hot. To hide her face, she walked over to the side of the pool and dived in, thinking the cooler water would help. Instead, the temperature rivaled the water in a bathtub. Ari would love it.

Zoe swam around while she watched Andreas carry Ari into the pool and put him facedown on the raft. He spoke to him in Greek. The love of father and son was something special to behold.

"Come and join us."

She moved to the shallow end and got on the other side of the raft. "How do you say 'Is it fun?' in Greek?"

When he told her, she imitated the words a couple of times, then asked Ari, who couldn't answer, but his smile did. "You do like the water, don't you?"

Andreas pushed him around and they worked together. "I think he's ready to try getting wet." He pulled him off the raft into his arms and started walking with him, splashing him a little bit.

Pretty soon he lay Ari against his chest with his face up so more water crept around his little body. Zoe stayed right with them as his daddy slowly swirled him this way and that. Ari let out a few nervous laughs, then reached for Zoe, who pulled him into her arms. He held her tight.

"Did that make you scared?" She kissed his cheek. "It's okay, darling. One of these years you'll swim rings around your father."

A smile broke on Andreas's striking face. He put his arms around both of them, taking turns kissing her and Ari. "I could do this all day."

"So could I," she said, giving him another peck on his hard jaw.

All three of them moved around the pool with Andreas holding them secure. Ari kissed his daddy several times. His sweetness touched her heart. This was a moment she would treasure her whole life.

After a few minutes, his son started to squirm. "I think maybe my boy has had enough for the time being."

Zoe handed him over to his father and they all got out of the pool. She reached for a towel to cover Ari, then plucked one for herself to dry her hair. Andreas put him in one of the lounge chairs and handed him a sippy cup filled with juice. He'd also brought out a banana, which Zoe peeled for him. He took a few bites.

"He's so cute I can hardly stand it, Andreas. I don't know how you handle the hours and days between visitations."

"I haven't done it well, but it's a fact of life I have to deal with."

"You do it superbly. He seems so well-adjusted. It shows he gets so much love from you and Lia. He's a very lucky boy."

"Do you know how remarkable you are to give her credit?"

She smiled at Andreas. "Why wouldn't I? Her lack of judgment cost her her marriage, but you can see she takes perfect care of Ari. Besides, how could I forget you fell in love with her, which means she has wonderful qualities? Otherwise you wouldn't have been attracted enough to marry her."

Lines darkened his face. "I wish I could be as generous about your ex-husband. I know he hurt you terribly."

"Some men just aren't ready for marriage. I've been thinking about Guion. Maybe he had to go through this experience to learn how priceless the right kind of love is. For his sake, and the sake of his wife and child, I hope he wins her back."

"Do you have any instincts over what he'll do about Ari?"

She shook her head. "Do you?"

"Lia asked me the same thing today. I told her I don't think he's going to want visitation rights. She's praying he doesn't so her parents will never find out. Which brings me to the one thing I haven't told you as a result of her coming to Patras."

Zoe didn't know why exactly, but she got a sick feeling in the pit of her stomach. "What is it?"

"To paraphrase Lia, 'I'll tell my attorney we're waiting to hear from Guion. Everything hinges on him should he decide to exercise his rights and turn this into a public scandal. After you bring Ari back on Sunday, don't plan to come to Athens again until his attorney talks to mine.'"

"Or?" Zoe prompted him. She was waiting to hear the rest.

"'I'll have a restraining order denying you visitation.'"

"So now this whole thing hinges on what Guion does or doesn't do."

"In her mind yes, but her stalling tactics won't work. The next step will be to inform her parents. That will end any problems with visitation. Once they know the truth, they'll refuse to pay her attorney fees. But I'd rather use it as a last resort."

None of this would be happening if Lia hadn't seen Zoe in Athens with Andreas. If she said as much to him now, he'd tell her they'd been over this ground before. That was because all roads led back to the starting point.

But what if Guion couldn't make decisions right now? What if it took him a month or more before Lia's attorney heard from him? Her jealousy could hold Andreas hostage in a visitation mess that could very well destroy him.

Zoe understood that he didn't want to tell Lia's parents the truth because he was such an honorable man. But there was something she could do—*she had to do*—and she put on her beach jacket.

"Andreas? While you deal with Ari and feed him, I'm going to go in and get cleaned up. After that I'll make us dinner."

"I think you'll find what you need in the fridge."

"I'm counting on it." She leaned over to kiss Ari's forehead. He was just finishing the last of his banana. "See you in a few minutes, cutie pie."

"Cutie pie?"

"Yes. With your phenomenal command of English, I'm shocked you haven't learned that endearment."

She heard his deep laughter while she headed for the guest bedroom to shower and wash her hair. After she put her jeans and top back on, she walked to the kitchen and found ingredients for omelets and salad.

In a minute Ari came in dressed in a playsuit and babbling in Greek. He walked over to her. Seeing someone here besides his mother had to be surprising to him. She looked down with a smile. "*Yassou*, Ari."

"*Yassou* to you, too." Andreas, so handsome it hurt, had just come in the kitchen wearing khaki pants and a sport shirt. He set the table and put on a loaf of the crusty Greek country bread she loved.

"Come on, Ari." He swung him in the high chair and gave him a piece of the bread and a sippy cup with some milk. "He'll eat what we eat."

Dinner turned out to be a riot. His son was very talkative, but it was unintelligible to Zoe. Andreas taught her how to say *ghala* for milk and *salata* for salad so she could practice on Ari. He squirmed a lot and kept saying one expression over and over. Zoe glanced at Andreas for a translation.

"He wants to get down."

"Ari shows all the signs of believing he's grown up and would rather sit in a regular chair. Look what you've got ahead of you."

"I *am* looking, and I love it." The way he was eyeing Zoe turned her heart over. It was time for her to leave.

"Andreas, I need to get back to the apartment."

His frown showed the first sign of tension. "I'm planning on you staying here tonight."

She shook her head. "You know perfectly well why I can't, so let's not talk about it again. If you'll send for the limo, or I can call for a taxi."

"Not yet. Ari wants you to play with us first."

For the next hour the three of them played hard on the floor in the nursery. Andreas got out one toy after another and they had wars until Ari laughed so hard he got the hiccups again. But he was getting tired.

"I believe he's as worn out as I am." Zoe stood up and started putting toys away while Andreas got his son ready for bed. Then she walked over to the crib. "*Kalinikta*, Ari."

She'd been practicing a few words to add to her vocabulary. As she started to leave the room, he called her name. It brought tears to her eyes she tried to hide before hurrying to the guest room.

Zoe tidied up and gathered her things into her bag. With that done she went back to the kitchen to clean it and put the dishes in the dishwasher. A sober Andreas walked in. "The limo is outside."

"Thank you for this wonderful day." She didn't dare say more. He was waiting to hear her tell him she wanted to be his wife, but she couldn't say it. Too much of his troubled life still lay unresolved. Nothing was fair.

He drew in a deep breath. "Tomorrow morning Ari and I will be by for you in my car at eight thirty. We'll have breakfast and drive to a great park for children. He loves going down the slides and sitting on the round top that whirls."

"I think with you he loves anything. What a joy he is."

Without actually answering him, she picked up her bag and they walked to the foyer. Once outside, he opened the rear door to the limo and helped her in. Before she could take a breath, he kissed her for a long time. When he finally relinquished her mouth, he whispered, "I dare you to get any sleep tonight."

"I haven't slept well since we met," she confessed, hearing the tremor in her own voice. "I love you, Andreas. Now you'd better go in. Ari might not be fully asleep and cry out for you. If he does, give him another kiss for me."

Don't look at me like that, Andreas.

To leave him was killing her, too.

He blew her a kiss as the chauffeur drove the limo away. The second he was out of sight, she phoned the Adonis hotel downtown where she'd first stayed until she'd found a bedsitter. They had a single room for one night. She booked it and told them she'd be arriving within the hour. But first she needed to pack her bags. Then she'd leave for the hotel in a taxi.

CHAPTER TEN

ANDREAS WENT BACK in the villa, but something wasn't right. Her *I love you* had sounded more like…*goodbye*.

He checked on Ari, who'd played so hard he'd passed out.

Without hesitation he pulled out his phone to call Zoe. She'd left her voice mail on. That wasn't like her. She would usually have answered after the first ring. A sense of dread swept through him.

After asking her to call him back, he rushed to the guest bedroom, fully expecting to find a letter telling him she was leaving Greece. He saw nothing!

Breaking out in a cold sweat, he went to his bedroom down the hall from the nursery to phone Gus. The private detective had left his voice mail on. Andreas told him what he needed and asked that he call him back as soon as he could. This was an emergency.

Frantic at this point, he raced to the kitchen to get a beer out of the fridge and call Yorgos. If he didn't answer, Andreas was going to lose his mind. It was quarter to ten, not that late.

The phone rang until he got a voice mail prompt. On a groan, he said he was calling with an emergency and didn't care if Yorgos phoned him in the middle of the night. They needed to talk.

While he paced the floor, Gus called him back, thank heaven. "I take it something serious is going on."

"Life-and-death kind. I need you to track down a five-foot-six dark blonde beauty named Zoe Perkins. She's a twenty-six-year-old American college professor who was staying at a apartment on Nikita Avenue downtown." He gave him the numbers. "By now I know she's left there in a taxi, or is planning to leave.

"I have every reason to believe she's going to

be headed for the airport on the first available flight. She could be flying to the US, Dijon, France, or possibly Venice, Italy. Her ultimate destination is Los Angeles, California.

"Gus—find her! Don't let her get away. She's my life!"

"I'm on it!" he exclaimed before hanging up.

He sat on one of the stools at the kitchen bar and called his housekeeper. Gaia had been with Andreas for the last five years. When Ari was born, she took perfect care of him at different times when needed. After she answered, he told her his dilemma. She assured him she'd come right over in her car and stay as long as he needed her.

"I might have to fly to Athens tomorrow."

"That won't be a problem. I'll be there in a half hour."

"Bless you, Gaia." She could sleep in the guest bedroom nearest the nursery.

Once he'd hung up, he phoned Zoe again knowing it was pointless, but he had to do something or go mad with frustration and anxiety.

Too restless to stay still, he finished his beer and walked through the house to look in on Ari again. Those hours that the three of them had been out in the pool had brought him such pleasure, he'd never wanted any of it to end.

By the time Gaia arrived, there was still no phone call from Yorgos. Andreas told her he might have to leave in the middle of the night and got her settled, then went to his bedroom. At eleven he heard his cell ring and clicked on.

"Yorgos? A lot has happened you need to know about. I was going to wait until Monday, but not now." After filling him in that Lia had brought Ari to Patras and the threat she'd delivered, he said, "I want you to call an emergency meeting with the judge tomorrow that includes Lia's attorney. The judge has to be told the real reason Lia keeps causing trouble. If you need me to be in court, I'll fly to Athens."

"I don't think your presence will be required. I have all the facts. With this new information I'll fax to his office tonight and to Lia's attorney, the judge should be able to decide quickly."

"He *has* to, Yorgos. When he learns about the lie and Lia's need to keep the truth from her parents, he'll have to rule on my terms of visitation. I'm through playing games and can't wait any longer. I'll convince the judge that although I may not be Ari's biological father, I'm his father in every way that matters."

"That should work. I'll press for him to render his final decision tomorrow, but I can't make promises for him."

"I know that, and I appreciate everything you've done."

"I'll contact you the second I hear anything."

After the line went dead, Andreas took a shower and climbed in bed. Sleep came in snatches. At five in the morning, he dressed in a crew neck shirt and jeans. With a check on his son to make sure he was all right, he left the villa and drove downtown to the apartment.

Maybe Zoe was still there, but not answering her phone. He waited out in front until seven, watching to see if she was leaving. When nothing happened, he went to her door and knocked. No answer.

In desperation he walked around to the manager's office. It didn't open until seven thirty. He waited outside where he could keep an eye on Zoe if she came out. Eventually a fiftyish-looking man came to the door and unlocked it.

Andreas went inside. "My name is Andreas Gavras. Here's my business card." He pulled it out of his wallet. "I've been trying to reach the American woman Zoe Perkins in flat seven. She's not answering. Would you ring her room?"

The man shook his head. "She checked out last night and paid her bill."

Though instinct had already told Andreas she'd gone, his heart still fell to his feet like a stone at the confirmation of his worst fear. "Did she leave a forwarding address?"

"I'm afraid not, but I could tell she was upset."

"Did you see her leave?"

"Sorry, Kyrie Gavras. Someone else came by

here last night asking about her and woke up my wife, but she'd already gone."

That would have been one of Gus's people. "Thank you for your help. If she comes back or gets in touch with you for any reason, will you call me at that number, please?"

The manager nodded before Andreas went back out to his car and drove to his office. Work was the only panacea while he waited to hear from Gus and Yorgos, but it was almost impossible to concentrate.

Zoe had probably taken a taxi to the airport and could be in the air right now headed for her apartment in Los Angeles. He didn't know her address there. In order to find her, he'd have to contact the English department at the university. But he wanted to catch her before she left Greece.

If he didn't hear from Gus soon, he'd phone the Decorvet estate in Burgundy and ask her friend Abby if she knew Zoe's plans.

She clearly thought that by sacrificing herself, it would appease Lia, but nothing could be further from the truth. The law would take care of that situation. Zoe was his life!

Come on, Gus. Find her for me...

Zoe spent a wretched night at the Adonis hotel while she sobbed for most of it. When she finally got up, she carried through on her plans to book a night flight to New York, and from there to Los Angeles.

Once that was done, she showered and left the hotel to get breakfast at a sidewalk café down the street. She took some hotel stationery with her to write a long letter in the sunshine to Andreas and tell him everything that was in her heart. It went on for pages because they'd done so much together and the memories kept pouring out of her.

At the end she wrote that she loved him, but knew it was best for him and his son that she leave Greece for good.

Around eleven she walked back to the hotel and posted it to his office address. She gathered up her bags and went down to the lobby to pay her bill. She asked if she could wait in the lounge and make a call before taking a taxi to the airport.

By now Andreas would have been up taking care of Ari for hours. This time with him was so precious. On Sunday he had to fly him back to Athens. Every parting had to be gut-wrenching for him.

It was gut-wrenching for Zoe. Just the thought of their having fun together without her started the tears again. She ached for him so terribly, she felt ill.

Andreas—how am I ever going to survive without you in my life? Everything is over.

"Kyria Perkins?" She lifted her tear-drenched face. It was the man from the counter. "Your taxi is waiting out in front."

She wiped the tears with the back of her hand before standing up. "Thank you for telling me. I can't believe it came this fast."

The man picked up her suitcases and followed her out of the hotel. Zoe looked for the taxi, but all she saw was a familiar silver Mercedes parked in front with the trunk raised.

Lounging against the side was the Greek god of her dreams come to life dressed in a crew neck shirt and jeans. Between the black fire in his eyes and a self-satisfied smile that said she could never get away from him, she almost fainted.

"*Andreas*—h-how did you know where to find me?" Shock and joy caused her voice to falter. She couldn't believe he was here, bigger than life.

"I have my ways. Don't ever think of trying to run away from me again, because I'll find you and bring you back every time. Let's go home and plan our wedding. The announcement has to go in the paper today so we can be married. My grandparents will be coming for dinner. They want to meet the woman who has turned my life around and brought the sunshine back."

Her heart was racing out of control. "What wedding? You're not divorced."

"But I am. I'll tell you everything in the car."

In the next breath he straightened and opened the front passenger door for her while the hotel clerk put her bags in the trunk.

In a daze, she climbed in. Andreas brushed her mouth with his before shutting the door. After he got behind the wheel and drove into the main stream of traffic, he grabbed her hand.

"I'm not letting go until you give me the answer I've been waiting for."

Zoe knew the question he was talking about, but her throat had swollen from all her feelings rushing in so that she could hardly talk. "You know I want to be your wife more than anything on earth."

"Will you marry me next week?"

A few minutes ago she'd thought it was the end of the world. "I'd marry you this second if we could. How did this miracle happen?"

"Yorgos met with Lia's attorney in the judge's chambers. Once he revealed her secret, the judge—disgusted by her flagrant lie—shamed her into signing the papers, giving immediate consent to the divorce.

"Even more, he promised to expedite the case through the courts so we can marry and honeymoon. It's still extremely quick, but we're going to get our hearts' desire. We'll also operate under the eight-day visitation arrangement until such time as more changes are needed."

"Oh, Andreas. I'm delirious with joy!"

"So am I. Now I'm going to give you another piece of information that's going to make you happy. Guion met with an attorney. Lia's attorney just heard from him. Norville has given up his parental rights to Ari with one proviso. That if there comes a day when Ari wants to get in touch with him, he has permission as long as it goes through the attorney and Guion's wife never knows about it."

The news caused Zoe to break down again. This time it was in pure gratitude for a prayer answered.

"You got through to him, Zoe."

She nodded and lifted a beaming face to him. "Somehow I know that one day Ari will have questions and the beauty of it is, he'll be able to approach his birth father, even if it's only for one time. Your son won't have to live his whole life wondering about the man responsible for bringing him into the world."

"It's a miracle, and *you* made it happen. At the lowest ebb of my life, there you were in that taxi, as if you'd been delivered just for me."

She gripped his hand tighter. "To be honest, I thought maybe the crash had made me hallucinate. The door opened and I saw my idea of a real Greek god who'd come to my rescue."

"What is this Greek god business you've referred to?"

"You have to be an American woman born in my time who always fantasized about a man like you. When my girlfriends and I were young, a Greek god was our idea of male perfection. It's the reason I was so excited to be assigned to Greece instead of Italy or France. Magda didn't have any idea how thrilled I was when we were told where we'd be sent."

His deep chuckle sent darts of delight through

her body. "I'm going to have to meet this Magda and thank her for sending you to me."

"She'll have a heart attack when she meets you. Don't be surprised if she asks you to be the leading man in one of her new films. I can promise that your female following will be legion."

"I only want one female in my life."

For such a renowned businessman, Andreas's modesty endeared him to her. "You've got me forever. I'm going to try to be the best stepmother in the world to Ari. I love him already."

"You're already winning him over. Did you notice how many times he kissed you in the pool?"

Oh, yes, she remembered, and nodded. "There's another blessing in all this, too, Andreas. Lia's parents never need to know what she's been terrified of them finding out. I'm sure they adore Ari and can go on loving him without her being afraid."

"A happier Lia will make life so much easier."

"I agree. She's a beautiful woman. One of

these days we can hope she meets a man she can love. But no woman will ever love any man the way I love you."

"Our honeymoon can't begin soon enough for me, Zoe. I need you in my arms and my bed nonstop. I'll ask Lia to keep Ari for two weeks. I'm going to need that long to believe you're actually mine. But I'm getting ahead of myself. Where would you like to be married, darling? Anywhere except Athens."

His first marriage had been celebrated there. "You mean out of all the beautiful places I've been while doing my research?"

"It's your decision."

"I'd consider it another dream come true to make our vows in that exquisite church in Santorini. The one with the blue dome and dazzling white walls. To me that's the closest place to heaven."

"Now I know we're meant to be together," he said in a shaken voice, twining his fingers with hers. "When I was eighteen, I worked on getting a hotel built there and visited the church you're talking about. It had a beauty I'd never seen anywhere else. A wedding was going on at the time and I decided I'd like to be married there one day."

She swallowed hard. "Are you serious?"

"I couldn't make it up."

"I know that. I'm just sitting here trying to take this all in, but I'm afraid it's not real."

"I promise you it is. Do you think your friends will be able to come? What about your adoptive parents and siblings? Would you like me to fly them over?"

"If we're getting married in a week, I doubt any of them could come."

"Then why don't we have our own private ceremony, and in a month we'll invite everyone to a reception at the villa. All the people we care about."

"That would be so amazing I can't comprehend it."

"We'll do it. Besides all my extended family, I have a few close friends through business I'll invite. You haven't met any of them yet."

"That's not surprising. You've been too busy putting your life together under the most painful circumstances."

In a few minutes he pulled up in front of the villa. He grabbed her bags and they went inside. This time as she crossed over the threshold, she realized this was going to be her home forever and she was going to be Kyria Gavras.

The housekeeper heard them come in. She and Ari walked into the foyer. Ari took one look at them and came running while he babbled their names. This adorable child was going to be her son. Forget the stepson business. When he was in her care, that's the way she would feel about him.

Zoe kissed him before Andreas swept him in his arms. "Zoe? Meet Gaia Salas. Gaia, I'd like to introduce you to Kyria Zoe Perkins from Los Angeles, California. Zoe? Gaia has been my housekeeper for years and I trust her with my life. I want her to be the first to know you have agreed to be my wife. We're getting married in a week."

The older woman put two hands to her mouth. "So soon?"

"It's not soon enough for me."

A broad smile broke out on her lovely Grecian face. "It's time you were happy again. I'm so happy to meet you, *kyria*." She spoke amazingly good English. That made Zoe happy.

"I feel the same way. Do you have family?"

"A husband and two children, both married."

"How about grandchildren?"

"Four. All are older than Ari."

"How wonderful. Do they live here in Patras?"

"Yes."

"I'd love to meet them one day."

"Thank you."

"Her family is always welcome here," Andreas explained. "Has Ari had his nap?"

"No. I was just going to put him down."

"If you'll do that, Zoe and I are going to be alone for a while."

"Desma will be here soon to start dinner. I'll help."

"Thank you, Gaia."

He kissed Ari and handed him to her. His son cried hard as she carried him down the hall. Andreas turned to Zoe. "This is one time when you come first. Let's take your bags to your bedroom."

"But he sounds brokenhearted."

"He'll live. I *won't* if I don't get you in my arms in about ten seconds."

Zoe decided he made it in nine before he pulled her down on the bed and then started kissing her close to oblivion. No kiss was long enough. They couldn't get close enough.

"You'll never know how much I want to make love to you." His voice was husky. "But we need all day and night alone."

"Darling—" she kissed him over and over again "—we have the rest of our lives. With your grandparents coming, and Ari, who might not take a nap after all, we don't have this luxury no matter that I'm dying of love for you. Didn't you say we have to get a notice sent to the newspaper today?"

"Yes. We'll go to my study to send it."

"I can't wait!"

"I don't deserve you, Zoe, but I swear I'll love and honor you all the days of our lives."

CHAPTER ELEVEN

THE FLIGHT TO Santorini took only an hour. Two limos were waiting for the wedding party when they landed. Another gorgeous, sun-filled day greeted Zoe as she left the private Gavras jet.

Andreas's grandmother Hebe, named after a mythical goddess, had gone shopping with Zoe during the week leading up to the wedding. After picking out her wedding gown, they decided on a stunning, eggshell-toned dress with a beaded hem on the elbow-length sleeves and neckline for her to wear to the Gavras hotel before and after the ceremony.

Hebe chose a soft pink, two-piece jeweled suit that went beautifully with her silver hair she wore swept back in a French roll. Andreas's grandfather Leonidas, a tall man with a lot of silver in his dark hair, wore a white wedding suit. The two made a striking couple and would serve as their witnesses.

Ari was back in Athens with his mother. They would see him when they got back from honeymoon.

Once the limos arrived at the hotel, Andreas carried Zoe's wedding dress to the bridal suite. "I'll see you at the church, my love. Are you ready to take my name?" His eyes almost impaled her with emotion.

For an answer, she kissed him hungrily. He could probably feel her heart jumping around with nervous excitement.

After she let him go, he disappeared with his grandfather to his grandparents' room to dress in his formal gray wedding suit. Within a half hour she would be married and had to hurry to put on her dress. Hebe helped her fasten the buttons in the back.

"You look a vision in this, Zoe."

"It is beautiful, isn't it?" She stared at the image in the mirror. The white tulle floor-length princess-style gown had an overlay of lace from the round neck and cap sleeves and down the bodice. Andreas had given her diamond earrings to match the round solitaire diamond ring set in gold he'd slid on her finger yesterday.

Hebe put a garland of white flowers in Zoe's hair. She didn't want a veil. "What's important is that you look beautiful in it. My grandson will be speechless when he sees you."

Zoe turned to her before going downstairs to the limo. "I love you already, Hebe. You couldn't know how thrilled I am to belong to your family."

Her brown eyes glistened with tears. "I wish my son and daughter-in-law were alive to see the kind of woman their son has chosen. I'd like to think they and your own birth parents are looking on today."

Now it was Zoe who teared up. "It's a beautiful thought."

"Shall we go? My grandson is waiting most impatiently to become your husband."

Together they went downstairs and out the foyer to the limo. The drive to the small, exquisite church overlooking the water didn't take long. The other limo was already parked there. How incredible that Zoe was going to be married here!

Tourists milling around stopped to watch as the driver helped her and Hebe out of the car and walked them up a lot of steps to the inside. Andreas had asked him to take pictures they posed for.

Then the doors opened and there was her husband-to-be, breathtaking in his gray wedding suit and silver tie against a white shirt. "You look so incredible, I'm in awe, Zoe."

"Then you know how I feel just looking at you." Their eyes clung while the driver took more pictures of the two of them before Andreas walked her inside. Leonidas was waiting and handed her and his wife a sheaf of white flowers. She kissed him before Andreas took her arm and walked her toward the front of the shrine. He'd explained that Bishop Dumitru of the Greek Orthodox Church would be officiating.

There was a spiritual atmosphere with the candles and the faint smell of incense that transported her to another world for the ceremony. After handing her flowers to Hebe, she joined hands with Andreas. She knew it would mean more to him if the words were said in Greek. Zoe didn't need to know the translation to imagine what was being said or the vows she was making. But he did speak in English when it was time for her to say "I do."

When the priest made the sign of the cross, Andreas took her in his arms. "You're my wife now, Kyria Gavras. I love you." With those words he kissed her. His fervency made her feel cherished. She'd never known a feeling like it.

He kept his arm around her waist and walked her out to the foyer, where the four of them hugged. Once outside the driver was there to take more pictures. More people had gathered round and clapped for them. It was very sweet.

"They don't even know us," she murmured to Andreas. He flashed her a smile to die for.

"This is a happy place and a lot of weddings are performed here. It will bring us luck."

"I don't need luck. I have you. I adore you, Andreas."

His eyes blazed with desire before they returned to the hotel. Once there, they enjoyed a wedding feast specially prepared for the present and former CEOs of Gavras House hotels. No luxury was spared to make it a day to remember all her life. But Zoe was too excited to be alone with Andreas to eat very much.

He noticed and whispered in her ear, "It's time." Andreas got to his feet. "My bride is tired. We're going to our room, and we'll see you tomorrow before we fly off on honeymoon."

Zoe stood up. "Thank you for making this day so perfect."

Andreas gave them each a kiss before ushering her out of the dining room and out in the hall to the elevator. She didn't know who was in a bigger hurry to reach the bridal suite. It felt like Zoe had been in love with him forever.

When they reached their suite, she removed

the garland and put it on a table with her flowers. Andreas took off his suit jacket and undid his tie. Next came his shirt. He tossed both on a chair. Little by little they left a trail, with the wedding dress being the last big item to be put aside before he carried her into the bedroom and laid her down on the bed. The covers had been turned down.

She heard an unmistakable sigh escape his lips before he covered her with his body and a new world opened up to her of loving and being loved like she could never have imagined. The pleasure they brought each other was indescribable.

They'd needed to be like this for so long, but the waiting had enhanced what they were sharing now. The freedom to show Andreas how much she loved him brought ecstasy. Near two in the morning he rolled her on top of him, covering her face and neck with kisses. He made her feel immortal.

"I hope we've already gotten pregnant," she

murmured against his lips. "One toddler isn't enough for us."

"I've been doing my best, *agape mou.*"

Zoe knew it meant *darling.* "If I conceive right away, our son or daughter will have a big brother. It's so fantastic to think about."

"Have I told you how delightful you are? How madly in love I am with you?"

"I can't hear it enough. Keep loving me, Andreas, and never stop. You're my whole world."

"Luckily for us we've got the rest of our lives to do this over and over again." So saying, he devoured her mouth, bringing rapture to her again. They made love again and finally fell asleep in each other's arms.

Zoe awakened after the sun's rays came through the slats of the shutters. Andreas lay beside her, looking at her. He needed a shave and had never looked so dangerous.

"You're so beautiful, I could look at you all day and night. Your skin is like silk. If I have one concern, it's that you're going to grow bored of me now that you've given up teaching."

"Maybe not," she said, kissing him passionately.

He raised up on one elbow. "What do you mean?"

"Do you remember the time you asked me why I'd gone over to the University of Patras?"

"Yes." He traced the line of her mouth with his finger. "You said you'd decided to talk to a professor about your research."

"I lied."

One corner of his compelling mouth lifted. "I'm intrigued."

"The dean of the humanities department offered me a temporary job to teach a section on Lord Byron this fall in their theater department."

"My brilliant wife."

"But you know why I turned it down. Maybe if I call him and tell him my circumstances have changed, he'll still allow it to happen."

"I have no doubt of it." He rubbed her arm as a prelude to making love. "I fell so hard for you from day one, I was afraid I would scare you off."

"Obviously you didn't. I wanted to be with you from that moment on."

Andreas wrapped a leg around hers. I'm so proud of my gorgeous wife, who not only has beauty, but brains."

She hid her face in his neck. "The thing is, if I get pregnant soon, I'll be able to teach and still have time to relax before the baby comes. If I don't get pregnant right away, then hopefully they'll want me to teach another unit. Barring that, I want to learn Greek and need to start lessons. Ari and I can learn together."

"Zoe—" He covered her with kisses and the world wheeled away until noon when they both awakened hungry.

"Don't move a muscle. I'll call for room service," she offered and reached for the phone on the bedside table. "I want to wait on you."

He lay back like a pasha against the pillows and waited while she told the kitchen what they wanted. Then she returned to his arms and he held her close. "After we eat, we'll have all afternoon to please ourselves. Tonight we'll go out on the boat and I'll show you more wonders you haven't begun to see."

She clasped his handsome face in her hands. "I hope you know you're the only wonder I want to look at or experience. Nothing else comes close to the Andreas effect. You come once in a millennium, and for some reason I still can't comprehend, I'm the woman who's been allowed the privilege to be loved by you."

EPILOGUE

Hollywood, California, a year later

"LADIES AND GENTLEMEN, tonight we're assembled here in the Galaxy Theater to honor Magda Collier and preview her extraordinary film about Lord Byron. Magda? Please come out onstage."

There was a thunderous ovation from a packed audience. Zoe looked around Andreas to smile at Ginger and Abby, who were sitting by their husbands. It was such an exciting night, the three of them were running on adrenaline.

The famous film director walked out to the podium, a flamboyant, much-loved character. The MC, the president of the screen guild, embraced her before stepping out of the spotlight.

"What a sight. All this distinguished body of

talent gathered together. Tonight is a landmark moment in my career. For years I've wanted to produce a film on Lord Byron, the great British poet, that shows him in a completely different light than the world has viewed him since the 1800s. I wanted him set apart from the usual clichés and I needed fresh material seen through new eyes. So I went to our great learning institutions to see if I could find these new eyes and discovered three outstanding scholars who came to Los Angeles to work with my screenwriters for a week. After I gave them their assignments, they left in January to begin their quests. As I say their names, will they please stand?"

Zoe moaned and grabbed Andreas's arm. Neither she nor the girls had any idea this was going to happen.

"The first scholar is Abby Grant Decorvet from San Jose State. She was sent to Switzerland to cover Lord Byron's travels there."

Abby got to her feet and had to wait several

minutes for the applause to subside. She'd given birth recently to a son. Both she and Raoul were ecstatic.

"The second scholar is Ginger Lawrence Della Scala from Stanford. I sent her to Italy, where the famous poet spent a great deal of time."

Another explosion of applause sounded as Ginger stood. Her friend was six months along and showing it.

Zoe got ready, because she knew she would be next.

"Our third scholar is Zoe Perkins Gavras from UCLA. She traveled to Greece, where Lord Byron's life was snuffed out at the age of thirty-six."

Andreas gave her hand a squeeze before she got to her feet. They'd just found out they were expecting, and her joy knew no bounds. More applause filled the theater. When it subsided, she sat down. It was a good thing since her legs felt like jelly.

"When you view this film, you'll begin to understand the brilliance of their research, which has been so divinely portrayed by the screen-writers and the actors for this film. It *is* a divine work, because George Byron was a genius. One thrilling side note for these three women is that all of them met the loves of their lives while working on this project. They married last year and now live in France, Italy and Greece, the three areas of Europe Byron loved so well. That was a bonus neither they nor I expected."

The audience laughed and clapped hard.

"And now…the film."

A hush fell over the theater as the movie began. Zoe sat there mesmerized, overjoyed, touched, moved to tears, haunted. The acting was superb. She experienced every emotion possible and knew the girls did, too, as they saw the beauty of Byron's poetry come to life on the big screen using the material they'd supplied.

Pride in her accomplishment brought tears to Zoe's eyes. Several times she glanced at the girls and noticed their eyes glistening, too. When she looked at Andreas, the love in his eyes melted her to the spot.

When the film ended, there was a roar of applause. Everyone got to their feet and cheered. Magda had to make six curtain calls. Zoe was so happy for the director, and humbled that she and the girls had been chosen to contribute to the making of such an extraordinary presentation. A masterpiece, really, from beginning to end.

As they exited the theater they were swamped by people who wanted to talk, to get an autograph, to take pictures.

A limo waited for them out in front and the six of them climbed in. Magda had booked them at the Kimpton Everly Hotel. When they arrived, they went up to Zoe and Andreas's suite to talk. No one would sleep for a while. There was so much to talk about they'd be up half the night.

Andreas ordered coffee and sandwiches, and they all got comfortable.

Ginger spoke up first. "I have to admit that I didn't expect the film to be such an emotional experience."

Abby nodded. "I know what you mean. Every time something new unfolded, I had to pinch myself to believe that the three of us were responsible for the information."

"It was really fantastic that Magda invited us and acknowledged us like that," Zoe murmured.

Andreas put his arm around her shoulders. "I know I speak for the men here when I say how proud we are to be married to such extraordinary women."

"Amen," they said in unison.

"I wish my brother, Gaspare, could have seen what we saw tonight."

"So do I, Vittorio," Ginger said to her husband. "Hopefully this film will be shown abroad and he'll have an opportunity to view it."

Raoul got up to pour himself another cup of

coffee. "The scene of *The Prisoner of Chillon* got to me." He eyed Abby. "The day we met, we went out on Lake Geneva and you quoted some lines to me. I'll never forget."

"Neither will I, darling."

Zoe reached for a sandwich. "Since we're going to be here for a few days, what do you want to do tomorrow?"

Andreas leaned forward. "Why don't we make the rounds to visit the places where our wives grew up?"

Everyone liked that idea, and then they decided to go to bed. Zoe smiled, because she knew the others couldn't wait to be alone.

After the others left, Andreas turned out the lights and they headed for the bedroom, their favorite place whether it be at the hotel, on the boat or at the villa.

Once in bed, he pulled her close. "That day when your taxi got in that accident I would never have dreamed we'd end up in Hollywood, attending a viewing of a film my wife helped make. After tonight you're a celebrity. It's a privilege to be married to you."

"I feel the same way about you." She started kissing him. "Let me show you."

* * * * *

LET'S TALK
Romance

For exclusive extracts, competitions and special offers, find us online:

f facebook.com/millsandboon

○ @millsandboonuk

🐦 @millsandboon

Or get in touch on 0844 844 1351*

For all the latest titles coming soon,
visit millsandboon.co.uk/nextmonth

*Calls cost 7p per minute plus your phone company's price per minute access charge

Want even more
ROMANCE?

Join our bookclub today!

'Mills & Boon books, the perfect way to escape for an hour or so.'

Miss W. Dyer

'Excellent service, promptly delivered and very good subscription choices.'

Miss A. Pearson

'You get fantastic special offers and the chance to get books before they hit the shops'

Mrs V. Hall

Visit millsandbook.co.uk/Bookclub and save on brand new books.

MILLS & BOON